Footprints in the Sand

Sandra Smiles

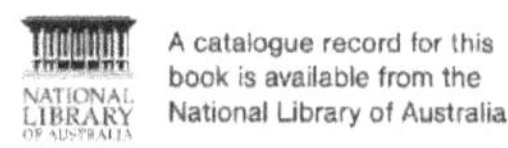

A catalogue record for this book is available from the National Library of Australia

First Edition: Maroon Star Doll, Rainy Days, Black Eyes, Denial and Ending published 2020 in Scribblers Anthology: A Year Disrupted
First Edition: Accidentally Dead published 2020 in Fun & Frolics, Rockingham Writers Centre 2020 Anthology
Second editions included in this collection

First published 2022 Paperback edition
Copyright © 2022 Sandra Smiles
All rights reserved.
ISBN-13: 978-1-922727-15-2

Linellen Press
265 Boomerang Road
Oldbury, Western Australia
www.linellenpress.com.au

Dedication

For Di, the wandering minstrel who chose
to settle with me

Contents

Foreword

I found a wad of folded paper and an old exercise book at the bottom of a box of photograph albums. I was surprised to find poems in various stages of bloom and a few short stories written by someone … none other than me.

I have always been an avid reader, but this unexpected find rekindled my interest in writing. I joined my local writing club, Scribblers Mandurah Murray Writing Group, and with their fabulous support, continue to develop my art. I soon joined The Society of Women Writers Western Australia and continue to thrive within the camaraderie and expertise offered by its members.

It is easy to put aside a short story with a thought that one day you will get back to it and turn it into a bigger project. Finding my scraps of paper suggested otherwise to me.

Writing a short story or poem is but one of many steps in a writer's journey. Rather than let any evidence of those steps be washed away by time and tide, I decided to create my own writing footprint in this collection. I have brought together updated works from my earliest forays into writing to the present day and added a few photographs. Not all are linked to the stories.

I invite you to step inside, explore and enjoy.

Maroon Star Doll

I originally started thinking about Arjun when I stumbled across information about Channapatna and the local art of making wooden toys. The original aim of my research was to find out about precious gems, particularly rubies. Maroon Star Doll grew from there.

The story was accepted by The Society of Women Writers Western Australia for inclusion in their Ruby Anthology 2021.

Word meaning: Bapuji: Uncle, the elder brother of your father (an alternative is Tauji)

Maroon Star Doll

My bapuji, Mr Bakshi, looked like a trussed goat with his arms and legs in plaster strung up with pulleys. The bandage at his fingertips, pink with blood, seemed to mock his effort to hold onto life. I felt more despair for myself than sorrow for my uncle. My resentment towards him has blinded me these last five years. Sitting here, holding my leather-bound book, I now understand and my heart is reaching out to him.

***

I, Arjun Basu, lived with my maa and baba in the outhouse of a large mansion in Calcutta. The abandoned mansion had fallen into disrepair. Families, looking to escape shop doorways and plastic bags, moved into habitable rooms. Soon a thriving community grew within its protective walls.

The day my life changed forever, I was waiting for maa and baba to return from Burrabazar Market. I was eager for their return, excited at their promise to buy Bengali sweets for me after I'd been diligent in my chores. A man walked into the courtyard, looked about and walked towards our home. Before he reached me, Mrs Naskar saw him, she saw everything.

I was certain she not only had a third eye but a fourth one at the back of her head as well. She bustled over asking what the stranger wanted, at the same time flapping her arms threatening to shoo him away.

Mrs Naskar calmed as he talked and kept looking at me. The stranger stopped talking, nodded at Mrs Naskar, turned and walked away. Mrs Naskar took me to her home where she told me my maa and baba wouldn't be coming back. A driver lost control of his bus, she explained. My maa and baba was at one of the street market stalls hit by the bus. They died along with many other people.

I stayed with Mrs Naskar until the day she told me I would be going to live with Bapuji. 'Mr Bakshi lives at Channapatna. I met him when he came to visit your maa and baba before you were born. I thought he was a kind, gentle man. I am sure you will like your bapuji, Arjun.'

What she didn't tell me was how the long the journey would be to Channapatna. Channapatna is a small village in the Bangalore district of Karnataka. Mrs Naskar put me on the train at Calcutta, where I lived for the first ten years of my life. I left with only the clothes on my back, a small meal of rice wrapped in muslin, and a bottle of water. The journey to Bangalore took more than a full day and a half.

Bapuji met me at the Howrah train station, he smiled at me and said, 'Welcome Arjun, you and I will be good friends.'

I recall my dismay at the slow, long and dusty, hours it took in Mr Bakshi's old Morris Oxford to Channapatna. I tried to stay awake and sat in sullen silence. Mr Bakshi kept a wan smile on his face, neither one of us knowing what to say.

Despite my tiredness hunger was an urgent desire when we arrived at Mr Bakshi's home. I bolted down the chicken and rice my bapuji put in front of me. I must have fallen asleep at the table as I woke the next morning on a mattress in the corner of the kitchen, with no memory of how I got there.

I lay still and quiet, seeing my maa's face smiling at me. *Up you get Arjun, off to school with you.* I could hear her voice. *We save paisa to make sure you get a good education, study hard, play can come later.*

Maa wouldn't let me miss school and I didn't mind, because I loved reading the history books in the school library.

My teachers fed my inquisitive brain. They would tell me; You will go far Arjun; we can't keep you supplied with enough books for your thirsty eyes.

Bapuji found me on the mattress with tears on my face. The memory of my maa and baba stung and gripped at my throat as I made a silent promise to apply myself to learn.

'When do I go to school, Bapuji?' I blurted.

'School? Bah!' he saw the shock on my face. 'No.

You won't go to school. I will teach you all you need to know.'

I felt sparks of rage, shocked Bapuji had dismissed my maa and baba's wish.

I ate breakfast in silence.

'Come Arjun, put away that long face. Here, my friends have given you new clothes. Hurry and get dressed, we have work to do,' Bapuji showed no heed to my sulking.

Ready, Mr Bakshi ushered me outside announcing, 'Today Arjun, you start to learn how to carve wood. You and I will work together.'

My anger flared. In my head I was screaming, I want to go to school! Consumed by anger I didn't understand what I was seeing when I stepped over the threshold. Toys surrounded me. Confused I stumbled further into the street, everywhere I looked I saw colourful toys.

'See Arjun, this is where we will carve,' Bapuji touched my arm and pointed to two tables and chairs under an awning. 'This is our workshop.'

On all sides wood carved dolls, whistles and puzzles were crammed on shelves. *How can this be, I have to work with stupid toys? Play should come later…*

I said nothing, lost in my anger and confusion, as he took my hand and led me to meet other stall vendors.

'Arjun this is Mrs Lal. She will help you make dyes

to colour the toys you make.'

Further down the street I met Mr Mangal, he would teach me about gems and where to find them. Mr Surat was the person who would sell us our wood.

Mr Bakshi created a routine for my life around teaching me carving techniques. He gave me the choice of what to make as I learnt how to carve. I chose whistles, which I soon regretted as I broke many pieces of wood before I got the hang of carving the holes.

I visited Mrs Lal every Thursday and she taught me how to make the dyes to paint the wood. Once every four weeks I went with Bapuji to visit Mr Surat to buy the best wood for our work. One day my bapuji told me I would be going away with Mr Mangal for a few days to see the mineral mines of Madikari.

Mr Mangal took me to the mines where I first saw a maroon star ruby. The deep, vivid red of the gem mesmerised me.

'Arjun, why are you bobbing up and down, craning your neck at such strange angles looking at the stone?' he asked.

'Look Mr Mangal, wherever you look at it, there is always a bright star shining from the centre.'

He laughed, 'That is how the light reflects in this precious gem, Arjun.'

Mr Mangal bought some gems. As we departed, he handed me a small bag. 'These are for you Arjun,' he explained. 'They are small off-cuts of the maroon star ruby you were looking at. The gem cutter saw you liked the gemstone, he told me to tell you these are its children.'

And on my life rolled in the rhythm of the routine.

For five years I kept asking Mr Bakshi to send me to school. 'Do I not give you books? Do you not learn anything here?' he would ask. My resentment grew every time he said no.

***

Yesterday, Mr Bakshi fell from a ladder. I had been holding it steady but stormed off, leaving him alone up the ladder, after another refusal for me to study. I went with him in the ambulance to hospital and stayed with him until doctors sent me home.

Next morning Mr Mangal roused me from sleep, 'Arjun, come tell us about your uncle.'

'Sit down child, tell us what happened and how is your uncle?' Mrs Lal asked as she sat me on my carving stool. Mr Surat stood in the background, his arms folded, watching me with a stern look on his face.

'I left him. He refused to allow me to go to college and study,' I explained. 'Bapuji kept working, the ladder toppled as he stretched to fix the roof. He fell over the fence into the next yard and dislodged a pile of clay bricks that cascaded onto his body.'

Our three friends looked sad. I saw Mr Surat nod

to Mrs Lal, then Mr Mangal gave her a curt nod.

'Today is your fifteenth birthday, Arjun?' Mrs Lal asked. I nodded and she continued, 'Your uncle gave me this so you wouldn't see it before today. Take it.'

She handed me a sandalwood box. Its surface covered by the carved intricate design of a large building. 'Open it Arjun,' she coaxed.

Inside the box was a leather-bound book and a pen. I picked up the book, perplexed when I flicked the pages and saw they were blank. A folded piece of paper fell onto my lap. I read it and asked, 'But what does this mean?'

Mr Surat was gruff when he spoke first. 'Have I not taught you about the history of the Persian artisans? Do you not know of the traditional ivory-wood they introduced to our forefathers? Do you not know where to find the best rosewood and sandalwood in India? Bah.'

Mr Mangal sounded exasperated, 'Have I not taught you about minerals and gemstones? Do you not understand about the subtleties of rock formation? Or where to find precious stones in India and other countries?'

'What about the vegetables?' Mrs Lal spoke in a quiet but insistent voice. 'Their special qualities in making colourful dyes? Do you recall our many conversations about spices? How India is the link between Persia and China in the spice trade? I know your uncle taught you about records and numbers in the keeping of his books.' Mrs Lal stopped and paused.

She cupped my face in her hands and said, 'Arjun, open your heart, not only your eyes and ears. Then, you will understand what you hold in your head.'

The note read 'Paper and pen for your studies'.

***

I am sitting in the workshop with my bapuji, he has helped me these last few months, during his recovery, to design a doll. We named it Maroon Star Doll. It is a student dressed with a graduation gown and carrying books. The original Maroon Star Doll, with a real maroon star ruby at the neck of the gown, sits at his right hand. He is laughing, his excitement catching as our friends gather around.

'Look, look. Here you are Mr Mangal,' he read. "Kings and royalty view the radiant red tones of the ruby as a symbol of strength, power, and wealth."

He is reading my words from 'Channapatna Dolls' by Arjun Basu.

Bapuji smiled at me, 'You and I will work together and be good friends' beta, my son?'

Music grew loud, the women started dancing and the men cheered as I replied, 'So we will baba, my father, so we will.'

Practical Seating

The writing prompt, Conundrum, set at a Scribbler's meeting, led me to set about having a go at writing a riddle.

A riddle is a verbal puzzle that can be in the form of a question, statement or phrase. The language relies on attributing strong imagery to everyday things. Many riddles can be written about the same thing.

Here is an example shared on many social media sites:

Only one color, but not one size.

Stuck at the bottom, yet easily flies.

Present in sun, but not in rain.

Doing no harm, and feeling no pain.

What is it?

Give yourself 30 minutes to see if you can work it out before you turn to the answer on page 20.

What Am I?

I was there at the beginning
and shall be there at the end.
Wielded through ages losing and winning
Against a foe attack and defend.
My orb of power unleashed and hurled
My portcullis strikes for your renown.
I am the centre of your world
forever at the heart of The Four Crowns.

Answer on page 139

Rainy Days

The first version of Rainy Days was first published in the Scribblers Mandurah Murray Anthology 'A Year Disrupted' in 2020.

Following is the second version, expanded for this collection.

Answer: A Shadow

Rainy Days

Jed let the Nissan ute crawl to a stop. Leaving the engine to idle, he scanned the valley ahead. A waterhole in its centre held a fair bit of water, a small solitary wooden shack stood to the north. Bob knew what he was doing putting the dam here. The low escarpment, undulating sand dunes and rocky outcrops with good pasture stretching south made this the perfect spot. And the Mallee trees provided welcome shade from the relentless sun for cattle. Jed saw none today, most of the herd driven to the northern paddocks for sale, a few kept near the homestead for breeding.

He nudged the ute forward. The rain would have been here two days ago. Enough to soften the earth and keep the indent of tyre tracks from two vehicles recently passed this way.

By mid-morning Jed felt the heat pressing on the vehicle windows. Another scorching day ahead.

Pulling up at the shack, he heard the frantic buzzing of flies before he saw them darting to and fro.

Jed gagged at the foul, sickly odour. As he approached the shack, the unmistakable smell of rotting flesh intensified. The door was ajar. He hesitated. *You have to check. Could be an animal. You'd look like a bloody idiot to get the police here for a dead cat. You know you have to look; don't disturb, don't touch anything. C'mon, get it over and done with.*

He pushed the door open. The flies rose as one from their feasting on the bloody mess protruding from a shirt collar. They surrounded Jed in an angry welcome.

He looked at the body slumped face down in the corner, partially covered with a blanket, one socked foot sticking out. He grimaced at the sight of bloodied hair with flies again settling, keen to resume their industrious feeding. His gaze took in a pair of gold decorated cowboy boots by the bed, with corduroy trousers dropped next to them on the floor. A glance around the one room of the shack before he closed the door, Jed noted two used cups, plates and a messy unmade bed.

Jed headed to the north track not far from the shack; it led to the homestead a two-hour drive away. He paused; climbed out of the ute, looked back at the valley, then turned and walked along the track. *Ah there it is,* he thought. A patch of red bulldust edged by rocks stretched for about 30 meters. The spot of many a bogging for unsuspecting visitors, especially after rain. He walked its length. The base had hardened, *not much rain after all.* Kneeling at the northern point, Jed brushed at the red dust and found a tyre track, with a faint but unmistakable tyre tread pattern.

Jed moved to higher ground and called the police on his Sat. phone and asked to speak to Detective Brian Johnson.

'Yeah, Brian, all okay with me and Mary thanks. Look, you need to get a team to the South Dam on the Wilkes' station. There's a body, covered with a blanket, in the shack. There are a pair of boots and trousers — they look like the style Bob Wilkes wears but I can't say the body, well, if it's Bob.'

'I'll get a team scrambled,' Johnson said. 'Jed, can you get to the homestead and I'll get there as soon as I can. Any other information?'

He gave Johnson a detailed account of the scene and what he knew from Val's radio call.

Val Wilkes had called yesterday, during the first good downpour of rain he'd seen for over a year. Jed smiled. He recalled how Mary, his wife, had run outside to rescue the washing. Slipping and slithering in the mud, she finally came to rest atop the tangle of now red, muddy sheets. Jed, coming to her rescue also fell foul of the slippery mud, laughing as he landed half on and half next to her. He grinned at the memory of the impromptu mud wrestling that followed.

'3 Oscar Lima, 3 Oscar Lima. Come in 5 Sierra Golf. Over,' Val's voice on the radio had cut through their laughter.

'I'll get it,' Jed said, staying on his hands and knees to get back to the radio.

'5 Sierra Golf, Jed here, go ahead Val. Over.'

Val explained her concern about Bob. He'd gone to the South Dam two days ago, Monday, and hadn't returned. Could Jed help and go make sure he was okay? She'd expected Bob to be home this morning.

This would mean a good three to four-hour drive for Jed, so he was curious why one of the boys couldn't go and check on their dad. He'd put the question to Val.

No, they couldn't help, she'd said. They had taken the ute and left for the Camp Draft on Monday morning. Bob went to the shack with the trail bike so Val was stuck and couldn't get there herself.

What about the housekeeper, Sharon?

As luck had it for Jed, another no. After the cattle drive, she had a week off to visit her family in the Alice. Bob had taken her to the roadhouse on Sunday in time for the bus pick up.

He suggested it might be better to call the police. Val said she felt embarrassed about calling the police, and besides, with Jed's experience and that she might be worrying about nothing, couldn't he do her a favour and check things out?

Jed retired from the police force a couple of years ago, but not before meeting Bob and Val when their twin boys, Matt and Pete, got themselves into trouble.

Jed helped get them back on track after what the boys thought had been a riotous prank.

He was reluctant but felt he had little choice and agreed to help. He'd left before sun up Thursday morning and made good time to the South Damn.

Jed arrived at the homestead to find Val waiting at the door, standing with her right arm wrapped tight across her chest, her left hand at her mouth as she watched him. She knew from his face he was about to confirm her worst fears.

'I'm sorry, Val, but I can't …' Jed said, reaching out to hold her as she fell to her knees. 'Val, I don't know what happened, I don't know who, well, who's body I found at the shack.'

'Oh, Jed, who else can it be?' Val whispered through her sobbing. 'Didn't you look? Couldn't you see it was Bob?'

'Come inside,' Jed said and guided Val to the living room.

'Look, I don't know who it is or what happened at the shack. The body was covered. I called the police, spoke to Detective Johnson. He's sending a team in the chopper to the South Dam. Val, have you seen or heard anything around here, anything out of the ordinary?'

'No.' She shook her head. 'Why? What are you suggesting?'

'I'm not suggesting anything. Like I said, I don't

know what's happened,' he said. 'All we can do is wait – let the police do their job. I'll wait here with you till they get here.'

Johnson radioed in the late afternoon that he was on his way; he arrived at the homestead at a little after eight. Jed made the introductions; Val provided cups of tea and sandwiches. Johnson looked at Jed and gave a little cough.

'Mrs Wilkes …,' he started.

'Please, Detective Johnson, call me Val.'

'Yes Mrs, err Val. Thank you, Jed, for calling in on the Sat. this morning – very timely it was too.'

He turned to Val. 'Jed reported he saw two vehicle tracks, two different tyre treads, at the south track. We have confirmed one tread is from your family's RAM ute. The second tread is from a trail bike tyre … again we have confirmed it is your family's bike.'

Jed reminded Val he had given the police the information she had given him during their radio call.

'And after Jed's call to the station, we checked a few of the details you gave Jed,' Johnson said. 'I need to ask you a couple of questions, Val, if that's okay with you?'

'Yes. Yes, of course, although I'm not sure what else I can tell you.'

'You told Jed Bob took your housekeeper, Sharon, to the roadhouse on Sunday.'

'Yes, they left after breakfast. Her mother hasn't been well, and Sharon wanted to go home and spend some time with her. With the boys away, this week worked for all of us.'

We had the police in Daly chat to Matt. He said Pete and Bob had an argument late Sunday afternoon, but Pete wouldn't tell him what the argument was about. Do you know what it was about?'

'Not really. I heard Pete ask his father something about the diesel. Pete organises the fuel orders,' she explained. 'He told Bob to pick it up after he dropped Sharon off for the bus to Alice. I thought they went outside to check the order and heard them arguing. I didn't think anything of it; they're very much alike you know … never happy with anything the other one does.'

'Do you know if Bob did pick-up the fuel?' Johnson asked.

Val gave a frustrated laugh. 'Well of course he would … ha! I bet that's the reason for the argument right there: Pete's found something to pick on about how many drums or how Bob's stacked them in the shed. Bob's slap-dash about things, not good with detail. I gave up nagging him years ago.' Val gave Johnson a wan smile.

Johnson nodded. 'So do you know how many drums he did pick up?'

'No, but they'll be in the shed. Do you need to

know how many?'

'Yes, I would, thanks,' Johnson said and added to Val's questioning eyebrows, 'Checking the details.'

Val nodded. 'Right.' She led them to the shed and pointed to where the drums were stored.

'There's only one there,' Johnson said. He went to the drum and tilted it. 'I'd say about half full. Would Bob leave the new drums anywhere else?'

Val had a puzzled look on her face; she shook her head, no.

Once back inside the house, the puzzled frown stayed on Val's face as she stared at the floor.

Johnson went on. 'Matt told us Pete dropped him at the Daly River Camp Draft but then left straight away. Pete told Matt he'd promised your husband to do an errand for him at the Three Ways. Do you know anything about that?' Johnson asked.

'Bob didn't say anything to me about an errand.'

'Mrs Wilkes, we confirmed with the roadhouse Bob didn't pick up the fuel. From what Matt told me it looks like Pete couldn't work out why Bob didn't pick up the diesel and wanted to find out. Matt thought Pete was angry and sounded as though he didn't trust Bob – he knows Pete was working up to tell your husband he wanted to run the station. Do you know anything about that, Val? Has Pete talked to you about it?'

'No. I had no idea …' Val looked confused now.

'Matt told us he could see Pete was looking for an excuse to leave him at Daly and told Pete to bugger off when he came up with an errand.' Johnson's eyes narrowed as he leant closer to Val. 'Have you noticed anything about Bob's behaviour lately that would cause Pete to not trust Bob?'

Val shook her head. 'No.' Her voice was flat, tired.

'Right. So can you think of any reason Pete would go to the South Dam?'

'What? Well, no. I thought he was at the Camp Draft with Matt. What are you saying, Detective? What's going on?' Val asked.

'The tyre tread imprint I found at the north track confirmed Pete had gone to the south dam on Tuesday, after the rain,' Jed said. 'Both the ute and trail bike were driven south sometime later.'

Johnson went on, 'We went to see your housekeeper, Sharon. On the way to her home, we spotted the ute. The driver was Sharon.'

'Sharon?' Val's head snapped up, her eyes pleading. 'How? I … I don't understand.'

'She hadn't gone home as you thought. Sharon told us Bob took her to the shack on Sunday. He didn't pick up the diesel because he didn't go to the roadhouse.'

'I … No. I don't understand,' Val stammered.

We have spoken to both witnesses and their stories are … almost, the same. At the shack, Pete confronted your husband. Bob got upset, angry Pete wouldn't listen and they fought.'

Johnson watched Val as he continued. 'Sharon said she tried to stop them fighting. There was a lot of pushing and shoving during the argument, then he fell and hit his head on the end of the bed. When he didn't move, they realised he was dead.'

'An accident?' Jed asked.

Johnson turned to Jed. 'They were fighting and it's still early days. We have to follow up on a few tests and procedures …' Johnson stopped short. He had been about to say they weren't convinced it was an accident but he registered the anguish on Val's face.

'Yes, it could be a tragic accident,' Johnson said. He focused a curious, intent look at Val. 'They admitted they've been together, in a serious relationship, for quite some time.'

Tears ran freely down Val's face now. 'But … I don't understand … why would they fight? Sharon's a nice girl. Bob … well Bob and I would have supported the two of them … Why would Pete go to these lengths? Why didn't he just tell us?' Val sat shaking her head a long moment.

'Are they at the police station … Pete and Sharon? What happens now?' she asked.

'Well, that's the thing, Mrs Wilkes,' Johnson said. 'We have Sharon and your husband in custody. Your son Pete is the one dead at the South Dam shack.'

Outback Track

In 2019 bushfires raged for 210 days across vast areas of the eastern states of Australia.

Volunteer firefighters, men and women, gave their all; too many gave their lives.

Families were torn apart; homes destroyed.

Wildlife, decimated.

In the midst of the catastrophe, the Prime Minister of Australia went to Hawaii for a holiday.

Denial

We watch in horror, the mad behaviour,
As nature succumbs, inferno is king.
The world on its knees cries out! Loud the ring
Of angry choir for a selfless saviour.
Death all around and politics waver
With meaningless words, a mocking grace sing –
An insidious debt is all they bring,
As frantic voices demand, 'Be braver!'
Rise up! Fight hard for what we need to be.
Strive to blow away haze of inaction.
Act now! Save our unique kaleidoscope,
Our planet, our country, our destiny.
Rise up! Deny regret its heavy traction
And dance in the joyous embrace of hope.

Mt Clarence Parklands, Albany. Field of Light: Avenue of Honour

Live

Live life to enjoy
strive learn aim higher
shun fear be connected
fly in love expected

Inky jealous times
new silly mistakes
days of dispute and fights
years of dislike and rights

From worry and pain
greed hurt despair
turn wanting and lust
to memories in dust

Enrich your senses
endure through it all
fossick bones of life's treasures
enjoy life's little pleasures

Black Eyes

I started writing about a boy and his dog. I didn't quite get it when other writers told me stories and characters have a habit of taking on a life of their own.

I get it now...

Black Eyes

Blackie shuffled to the door in time to aim his rifle at the bare feet scrambling behind Smithy's water tank. His eyes struggled to focus across the rifle sight. He moved the gun barrel along the tin corrugations, expectant his quarry would emerge at the other side. Though whiskey mussed from last night's binge, he had enough sense to lower the rifle. Jaw clenched and growling an old drunk's mutterings, he went back inside. Mila stopped shoving clothes into a black rubbish bag and moved towards the door.

'Where d'ya think ya goin'?' Blackie slurred.

Mila took in his battered, worn features. Long gone was the tall, cocky stance of his lithe body, work-hardened by pick-and-shovel mining. His black curly hair was now an uncombed grey mess. A food-stained filthy beard covered his sallow face. Once sparkling blue eyes, now grey and cold, bore into her.

Mila dropped her eyes and turned to leave.

Snarling like a wounded bear, Blackie threw himself at Mila's back, grabbing at her clothes. Mila stumbled forward towards the doorway; her head banged against the wall. She reached out, grasping for anything to stop her fall. *I have to get out. Get out. Run. God, he's gonna kill me this time. Run. Run …*

Driven by drunken rage, Blackie picked up a wooden chair and hurled it at her. The effort propelled him forward. He fell, knocking himself out on the bare wooden floor. Minutes passed. He came to in murky confusion, his drunken rage abated. He lay still, imagining Mila watching him, doing as he said, like she always did. He pushed himself onto his side. Mila lay motionless across the threshold. He crawled to her; grabbed her hair; attempted to lift her head. His hand slid on the back of her skull.

Blackie wiped his bloodied hand on her dress. He propped himself on the door frame and stared past Mila's body to the opal mullock heaps beyond.

Earlier that morning

The population of Brookslake is sparse, but enough to support a general store and primary school. There are two pubs and the odd opal find that sustains a police station. The locals refer to red dust tracks as streets. The main street, a dry, rocky creek bed, turns into a raging torrent when it rains, flooding the few shanties hugging its banks.

This morning Toby is in bed, his eyes closed tight, knuckles at his mouth hiding his smile. A wet sloppy tongue licks his ear and his resolve melts. 'Happy birthday, Odin, Happy birthday!' Toby threw his arms around Odin's furry neck.

Toby had spotted a small ball of rusty red fluff the last time the main street flooded two years ago. The puppy was shivering, scared, looking for shelter. Its black eyes fixed on Toby, pleading for help. He'd wrapped the dog in his jacket and named the dog Odin, as it was Wednesday, Odin's day, the father of his hero Thor.

Odin felt Toby's excitement and leapt off the bed to retrieve his toy. Mila opened the bedroom door a crack, slipping in to see Toby and Odin in a tug of war with an old piece of rope.

'Out of bed, Toby,' Mila said. 'I know it's Odin's birthday but you still have to go to school.'

'Shut up. Get out. I'll shoot that bloody dog!' yelled Blackie.

Odin slunk low, growling. Wide-eyed, Toby shook, for a moment trapped in shock and fear. *What did we do wrong? Why can't you leave Odin alone, he hasn't done anything to you. Why do you hate him? Why do you hate me?*

'Come on, hurry. Get up,' Mila ushered Toby. 'Shoo, Odin,' she said, pushing the dog to the open window.

Odin jumped out, as he'd learnt to do in the first few months of his life. And, when Blackie banged into chairs, when the table scraped on the bare wooden floor, as he stomped towards the bedroom, Toby had soon learnt to follow the dog ...

'Where's that bloody dog?' Blackie shouted.

Toby grabbed his school clothes and swung onto the window ledge. His head snapped around as the bedroom door slammed against the wall. He saw Blackie aim his rifle. Toby jumped and ran, Odin at his heels.

Boy and dog reached Smithy's water tank and scrambled out of sight. Toby held and hugged Odin. 'I won't let him hurt you, Odin. I won't.'

Later that afternoon

Toby didn't have a good day; he'd had a fight with Lucas Becker, his second cousin. Lucas taunted Toby. He sang in his smarmy sing-songy voice, 'Toby's a bastard, a dirty stinking bastard. Where's your homework, Toby? Odin's got fleas …'

Still angry with himself, ashamed that he'd run out of the house scared, Toby's deep blue eyes darkened to black. His single punch floored Lucas. Toby spent the afternoon in the headmaster's office, waiting for his mother to come and get him. Worse, he was sure that Sergeant Becker, Lucas's dad, would turn up and give him a bollocking, or worse.

When the bell rang, putting a full stop on the end of another school day, Toby went home; his mother hadn't come.

Anger, outrage and hatred for the old man fueled his legs as he ran home. He burst through the front door. Stopped short.

Blackie sat looking at him through beady, cruel eyes. 'Ya mother's gone.' He stood up and shoved his way past Toby, picked up his rifle, mining pack with knotted shaft rope, water flask and left.

Toby watched Blackie throw his pack into the ute and drive off; watched till the dust cloud settled. He scratched his black curly hair. Not knowing what to do – no food in the cupboard – he took himself to the bedroom he shared with his mother and lay down. His bed under the window, hers empty on the opposite wall.

Thursday

Toby jolted awake from his fitful sleep, a cold muzzle on his face. 'Odin, you're alive,' he cried.

Odin licked Toby's face and pulled at his shirt collar. Sitting back on his haunches, he barked at Toby, then turned and jumped out the window, disappearing into the diffused grey, pink light of dawn.

'Odin, come back! Odin.' Toby shouted. *Odin, don't leave me alone. Come back; I'm scared, Odin, please come back.*

Toby started to cry and whispered, 'You said you would never leave me, Ma.'

He lay for a long time, remembering other days when he came home from school. His ma would be waiting with Odin at Smithy's water tank so she could walk the rest of the way home with him. He would run to her and she would give him the biggest hug and tousle his hair.

His memories shifted to the days she wasn't waiting. Those days he would creep into the kitchen where he found his ma crying. She used to smile at him through her tears. He would hug her and hold on tight, confused at her pain, and then go to bed hungry for something other than food. Toby shuddered at the memory of the last time he had seen her like this. He had made too much noise, and Blackie had whipped the back of his legs with a thick leather belt.

He jumped up and looked out the window. The sun was now high in the sky. *Odin is with ma!* he thought. Then he yelled out, 'I'm coming to find you.'

Only one place to go. Toby filled his water flask and ran off, past the mullock hills into the red gibber plain. He would start at Old Jack's Claim, his and Odin's hangout.

Jack had taught Toby a lot about opal. He understood Blackie obsessed about finding black opal.

'He's a fool!' Jack had exclaimed. 'In these parts, it's all light. Still has flashing fiery orange, green and red colours. But that vibrant deep red set in black is further north. Anyways it gave 'im his name. Blackie's a helluva lot better than Walter Schimmel,' Jack would laugh.

Toby reached the hangout and set about checking his few belongings for a packet of potato chips he thought he had left there the other day. Torch, small shovel, a sleeping bag and a few Thor comics, no chips. He decided to read his favourite story to take his mind off being hungry. He was sure Odin would come, so he waited. Night time started to close in.

The door swung open, startling him.

'What're you doing here?' he asked of Lucas Becker.

Lucas stood there, shaking. Dingoes howled in the distance. He attempted to explain, 'Dad told me to apologise for calling you names, said I deserved the punch.' He shrugged. 'Mrs Smith said she saw you heading here earlier, so I came to check.'

Dingoes let out another mournful howl and Lucas's eyes grew wider, 'Can I stay? It's getting dark.'

They settled in an uneasy truce.

Friday

Scratching at the door woke both boys.

Lucas scrambled next to Toby. 'What was that? Might be a dingo?' he whispered.

More scratching. This time with another noise, a sharp yip. Toby jumped up and opened the door. His face lit up when he saw Odin.

Odin nuzzled Toby; his tail wagged his delight. He barked at Toby, ran off, stopped, barked. *Follow me.*

'C'mon Lucas we have to follow him,' Toby shouted. He grabbed the torch and water and took off after Odin. Lucas didn't argue, not wanting to be alone.

Odin circled Old Jack's claim and disappeared into a crevice. It took the boys a while, but they cleared rocks and debris to make a hole big enough to slither through.

Toby swished the torch beam, whispering to Lucas, 'Looks like an abandoned mine tunnel.'

They shuffled on their bellies till they came to a small hollow, and rested on their knees to get their breath. Lucas heard it first, the unmistakable sound of someone using a pick. Toby turned his torch off, dropped flat and crawled his way toward the sound. Lucas hesitated, scared, reluctant but didn't want to be alone, so followed Toby.

The tunnel widened, and a dim light came from a cavern ahead. Toby gasped. A figure wielding a pick, and Toby knew before he saw his face: *Blackie.* At the shadow's edge, he saw Odin crouched next to a bundle of clothes. His mum's clothes. Toby prepared to leap into the cavern but Lucas grabbed his shirt and pulled him back.

'Who's there?' called Blackie. 'Show ya'self.'

Lucas whispered, 'Shh. He can't see us.'

Blackie stood listening for long moments, then returned to his digging.

Lucas, shocked at what he'd seen, pulled Toby back to the hollow, where they devised a plan. They pumped fists and crept back. The cavern light had gone, and so had Blackie.

Toby retrieved his torch and scrambled to his mother's side.

'Is she alive?' Lucas asked, peering into Mila's face.

'Wouldn't ya like to know,' Blackie growled, stepping out of the shadow. His rifle pointed straight at them.

Toby stood rigid. His eyes blackened, reflecting vibrant red shards from the torchlight, glaring at Blackie.

The old man gasped; taken aback. He lowered the rifle to his side. Toby's eyes. Black opal, his treasure.

Then Blackie came to his senses, aiming the rifle once again at Toby. Odin leapt from the shadows and clamped his jaws on Blackie's arm. He held on till Blackie dropped the rifle to fend him off. Odin yelped as he hit the cavern wall, then fell silent.

It gave Toby time to snatch up the gun. He cocked it; pointed the barrel at Blackie. So many times, he had seen Blackie do this to make any mistake now.

Blackie laughed, 'Ya haven't got the guts to shoot me. Ya like ya ma, scared of ya own shadow.'

Not anymore! thought Toby, his eyes watching every move Blackie made. His finger twitched on the trigger.

'Besides, ya haven't got the heart to shoot ya own father.'

My father? Toby heard himself say, 'You know my father? Who's my father?'

'I'm ya father. Ya ma's a whore,' Blackie gloated.

'You're a liar!' Lucas shouted. 'Mila's your daughter. You can't be Toby's dad.'

'Ahh, the other runt can speak,' snorted Blackie. 'Wouldn't yell too loud, son.'

'Don't call me son,' shouted Lucas.

'Why not? Gunna get yer dad onto me? Can't see 'im here.'

Then Blackie lunged forward, trying to wrest the gun away from Toby. Lucas charged at Blackie from the side, knocking him off balance and dropping him to his knees.

Blackie held his arms wide, 'Go on then. Shoot me.'

Lucas saw Toby steel himself and start to squeeze the trigger.

'You don't really wanna do that, Toby,' urged Lucas, 'Drop the rifle. I'll tie his hands and legs.'

Lucas had the miner's rope and wrapped it around Blackie's neck before he could react. He then looped and pulled it tight around his ankles.

Toby stared at Blackie across the rifle sight, at the monster of his waking hours. He sucked in a deep breath, squared his shoulders, and lowered the rifle. He looked over at Lucas, who gave him a lop-sided smile. Blackie let himself fall on his side and lay like a trussed wild animal.

Lucas scrambled off to fetch his dad.

Odin limped to Mila and licked her face as Toby sat

by his mum, 'I love ya, ma. I'm sorry I …,' he stopped and shed silent tears. He cried for his ma. He cried because he felt ashamed, empty and lonely.

Odin put his head on Toby's lap as if to tell him, *You're not alone.*

They waited in silence. Two hours seemed like an eternity before Lucas got back.

'Good lad, Toby. I'll take that rifle,' Sergeant Becker said. 'C'mon, Toby, come with me.'

Toby took Mila's hand to have his last final moment with her. He couldn't be sure, but he felt again the slightest of pressure close around his fingers. Then he was shouting, 'Sergeant Becker, she's alive. Her hand … she's moving her hand.'

Odin went to Mila and licked her face, his furiously wagging tail matching Toby's joy and excitement.

Remnants of a Time Past

Ending

Time is slowly ebbing,
Hours ticking by.
Serenity surrounds me,
Peaceful as I lie.

Time is closing in,
Minutes seem so short.
Memories enrapture me,
In the past I'm caught.

Time is almost gone,
Seconds trickle by.
Pain stops haunting me,
Quiet and still I lie.

Time stops passing.
No sound is heard.
Air hangs still and heavy.
Gone on wings of a bird.

I didn't mean to kill the ball ...

Accidentally Dead

I lay awake, taking in the minty pine aroma from the eucalypt and the rich earthy smell of its fallen leaves. *Happy birthday, Jenny, 29th February.* I couldn't help but grimace at the memory of two leap years ago when I hosted a weekend birthday bash. Prepare for a few surprises, I told my guests. The one surprise no one expected, including me, was my death.

Feeling a subtle rise in the warmth of my surrounds, I sat up, turned my head and came face to face with a brown-eyed, black, hairy terrier, leg cocked, delivering one of its many morning p-mails to my head stone.

'Leroy! Leroy! Come away from there,' his master called.

Leroy started a low rumbling growl. *He can see me.* I leant to look over Leroy's shoulder. *Master doesn't seem to see me.* He kept walking past my grave, waving a treat to lure his dog.

'Leroy. Come away from there. The relatives of that poor soul won't appreciate you peeing on the marble.'

Bugger the relatives. What about me? 'Shoo, you lousy mutt,' I whispered while wafting my hands in front of the dog's face. One last growl and Leroy trotted off. *Hmm, that worked well.*

I stood up and stepped out of my eight by two-and-a-half-foot plot onto the grass. My hands fell from a long body stretch to automatically brush my clothes. Looking down my front, I saw I was wearing my blue business suit and white shirt; they were neither creased nor dirty. Definitely not wet. *At least my ghostly self doesn't have to worry about doing the laundry.*

I gazed at my headstone:

Jennifer Smith

1984 – 2012

Daughter of loving parents Harold and Yvonne

Beloved by Family

Cherished by Friends

'Died at the Hands of Friends' more like it.

A cough. 'Good morning, Jennifer.'

Startled from my reverie, I turned to see a grey-haired old lady, her hands clasped, smiling at me. Taken by surprise, I glanced left and right. 'You can see me?'

'Yes, dear. Forgive me, but I saw you last time you rose, but I thought it best to stay out of sight,' she said.

'What? Stay out of sight? Who … you can see me?' I realised I was babbling. 'Who are you?' I eventually blurted.

'I'm Sadie Hancock. Three graves down across the path,' she pointed to her plot. 'The one with the small spire. It's nice, don't you think — not too long and spindly like some others in here. Mind you, it only went up after Arthur died. I was surprised,' she mused, 'nothing went up when he was alive.'

She saw my eyebrows shoot up and quickly changed the subject. 'Oh look, what a lovely pot of flowers, gerberas, I think.' Sadie picked up the pot of flowers my mum had left. 'Why did she leave them yesterday, dear? I assume you died on this date, given you're rising on the same day you did last time?'

'Yesterday was my birthday. Well, it's really today, my birthday, that is. Mum picked the 28th February and Dad the 1st March when it wasn't a leap year.' I smiled. 'I caught on pretty quickly, so each leap year turned into a three-birthday bash.'

'Ah, and you died on your real birthday in 2012?' Sadie asked. I nodded. 'But why are you still here?'

'I was killed by a friend at my birthday party.'

Sadie looked horrified. 'A friend murdered you?'

'No. No. I wasn't murdered. Well, let me explain.'

I recounted the story of my 29th February 2012 birthday and how the upcoming London Olympics had spawned numerous conversations around Usain Bolt, the fabulous Jamaican sprinter. I smiled, and told how we decided to conduct a sprint competition: 10cms with a worm each – first past the post and winner takes all. At the count of three, we tickled our worms to see them hare off into the underbrush from whence they came.

'To this day, the race hasn't finished,' I said, and we both laughed. 'The party was swinging into evening when I walked into the room just as Tom was doing a "Bolting pose". I ducked to avoid Tom's leading arm but met the champagne bottle Mary was waving about. *Anyone for bubbly?* was the last thing I heard as I fell forward and before my temple cracked onto the corner of the beautiful and quickly blood-stained French marble coffee table.'

'Oh my …,' Sadie exclaimed.

We both turned to the noise of crashing and rustling leaves from the Eucalypt.

Oh no. I thought. The Abster has arrived.

'I'm sorry, just give me a minute. Flight feather caught the branch … Arrgh …' she yelped and tumbled from the tree but still managed to land on her feet. She fluffed her feathers before resting her wings and greeting us, 'Hi, Sadie. Jenny, I'm sorry I wasn't here when you woke up.'

My guardian angel Abigail.

'Hi Abby, any news for me?' I asked hopefully.

She shook her head. 'Jeremial is still upset with you.'

'Oh, I know,' I sighed loudly. 'He's told me numerous times how I've thrown the universe out of whack. He flew off in a huff last time I saw him.'

The Abster chuckled. 'He can't help you cross over to the spiritual realm and it's sent him into a tailspin.

He's still trying to latch onto the cloud shimmering just out of his reach.' She grinned at me. 'He hates that, and you know Jerry does everything by the book.'

I grinned back and circled to lean on my gravestone, 'Tell me about it. He even complained to Uriel. Not that it did him any good. Uriel said he can't do anything about it. I still don't get it, mind you. I thought angels could do anything.'

The Abster glided to my side and put a comforting arm around my shoulders. 'Your multiple birthdays have thrown out the balance of the universal spiritual waves. Now the only way the spiritual bridge to the other world can be accessed is if someone you know dies on the same day, as close to the same time, as you did.'

I groaned. 'What are the chances? We're talking about a leap year, every four years, and I'm supposed to find someone willing to die.'

'Well, dear, you're not alone. Jeremial told me the same thing,' Sadie said. 'The excuse he gave me is because I killed myself, mistakenly mind you.'

'Mistakenly killed yourself?' I asked.

'It was Arthur's fault. He didn't drink the tea, you see?' I told Sadie I didn't see.

'Oh, he was obsessed with his bloody trains. That's all he did, play with his train set. I decided to get rid of him and his trains. I made him his morning tea and he told me to put it on the Flying Scotsman's carriage. I sat down waiting for him to stop the bloody train and drink it. I sat there so long that when the Scotsman chugged by me for the umpteenth time, I picked up the cup of tea and drank it. I forgot I'd popped in all the insulin I'd picked up from the chemist, the whole lot. I simply went to sleep and the old fool didn't notice me until he went looking for his dinner.'

Abigail interrupted. 'Look, Jenny, Tom is coming.'

We all turned to watch Tom walk towards my grave, flowers in hand. As he drew close, we could see he was chewing on something but his face took on a puzzled look, then shock.

I looked at Sadie and realised she was still holding the pot of flowers from my grave. To him, it would look like they were floating in mid-air.

'The flower pot,' I yelled.

She immediately dropped the pot and it smashed to pieces as it hit the ground. That did it. Tom gasped, his hand shot to his throat, he dropped the flowers, fell to his knees for a long moment, then keeled onto his back.

'Oh my God. He's choking,' I screamed, running to his side.

I automatically knelt and tried to compress his chest but I wished I hadn't, as my hands went through his chest into the earth below. I just stopped my momentum with my chin on his chest. I pulled back. *Aww yuk,* I thought, *I nearly saw the inside of him.*

'Abigail, Sadie, help him,' I yelled.

Abigail lowered her head, 'I am forbidden to interfere.'

Of course. 'Sadie,' I shouted. 'You can pick things up … come on, you'll be able to hit his chest.'

'Right, right, hit his chest,' she said. 'Hit his chest …'

I turned to see why she was taking so long.

'Noooooo!' I screamed. 'Put that down. Hit his chest with your hands, not a bloody gravestone.' She dropped the gravestone.

Sadie got next to me on her knees, her hands flapping above Tom. I reached over, grabbed them and pushed them down onto his chest. He coughed and spat out a gooey mint lolly. He took several rasping deep breaths and gradually sat up.

Oh no. Too late. 'What have I done? Damn! If he'd died, I would be free,' I cried.

Abigail looked horrified at the thought.

Tom stood up, looked at the broken plant pot and gravestone and took off.

'No. You're right,' I said, looking at Abigail and then Sadie. 'It's not his time.'

'Ladies,' Jeremial announced his arrival.

I turned on him, 'Do not do that. You'll be the death of me one of these days.'

Everyone looked at each other.

'Okay, okay,' I said. 'Good to see you, Jeremial.'

'You both must come now; you're sharing a cloud, and it's ready,' Jerry beckoned to us.

Abigail smiled at us and explained, 'You wanted to save Tom's life, not see him die. You are both free to leave.'

I stepped forward and fell over the broken gravestone. *Can't touch anything but I can fall over a gravestone...*

I looked up and saw Leroy was back and peeing on my headstone again. I smiled at Abigail, took Sadie's helping hand and we followed Jeremial towards our cloud.

Suddenly, Sadie started to try and pull away.

'C'mon, Sadie, there's nothing to be scared about,' I said.

'Yes, there is. Look ...' She pointed to the cloud.

Peeking over the edge of the cloud was a man, smiling and waving. In each hand, he held a model train.

Sunset Light

Storm Brewing

Collie Well Charm

The sun's first rays cast an orange glow over Hartley Bay. The tall towering cliffs of St Mary's Island, a stately backdrop to the silhouette of the oak tree, misshapen and bent from years of struggle against sea winds, stood proudly on the promontory of the mainland coast. The makeshift noose, strung on the oak's thickest branch, swayed in the early morning breeze, the latest warning from Lord Hastings of what to expect if the new tax wasn't paid on time. The tide was out. The causeway to the island, and the rocks between the mainland and the island, now visible, as were local fishermen, their backs bent catching their bait for the day from the rock pools.

'Howway, Jenny. Da said we could go home and have breakfast at sun up,' Irene, Jenny's sister, whined. 'Take me home, Jenny. I'm hungry.'

'Whisht ya gob, Irene,' Jenny snapped. 'We have to help Da or he'll be in trouble with Hastings. You know he told us he needed a big catch to raise money for the new tax.'

Irene let out a big sigh but bent over and continued picking whelks and winkles from the water. Some, she knew, would be used in the soup for dinner.

Jenny noticed a handsome young man clamber onto the rocks. She watched him pick his way to the causeway and onward into the Benedictine Chantry, the only building on the island. She knew it was William, Lord Hastings' only son. She shook her head and thought about the young William who used to visit their home, even staying some nights so he could go fishing with her da the next morning. He and Jenny often played together, laughing and running along the beach, even collecting whelks in these very rock pools. Not long after his mother died, he stopped visiting. Lord Hastings kept his son close; maids from the castle told tales of Hastings' too frequent beatings of William.

William grew into a surly young man. Locals were as scared of William as they were of his father. Jenny was careful to move away if she saw William approaching. On the odd occasion he caught her eye, she gave a curt nod which he never acknowledged – he just stared at her and watched her leave. Her da, Jim Dodd, had the knack of drawing Lord Hastings' wrath. The villagers listened to Jim, and Hastings didn't like that at all.

'Look, Jenny …' Her sister dragged her from her thoughts. 'Look, Collie Well. Howway, I dare ya. Look into it and say the charm.' Irene gazed into the mirror of still spring water, her face smiling back at her.

'Don't be silly, Irene. It's an old witches' tale. Why

do I want to see my future husband's face?' Jenny bent to pick up more winkles.

'Well, why did ya learn the charm then? Howway, show me how to do it,' Irene cajoled.

Jenny couldn't deny she was curious.

'C'mon, Jenny, it is St Agnes Eve. Please,' Irene pleaded.

'It might be St Agnes Eve, but it's first thing in the morning – the charm only works at midnight.' She looked at Irene's sullen face. 'Oh, all right,' Jenny said, bending to look into the well. She chanted:

"Agnes sweet, and Agnes fair,

Hither, hither, now repair:

Bonny Agnes, let me see

The lad who's to marry me.'

Jenny was about to straighten when a face appeared. Her hand shot to her mouth as she gasped. She turned around, 'Alan Curry, what're you doing here? Scared me nearly to death, you did.'

Alan was laughing. 'Forgive me, Jenny, my bonny lass. I saw you and had to come and say hello. I didn't expect you'd be singing into the well.'

'I wasn't! Irene wanted me to look at something she thought she saw,' Jenny replied with an indignant air.

'Jenny, Irene. C'mon home with you both. We've done well and ya ma'll have breakfast on the table,' Jim called to his daughters.

Alan took Jenny's elbow. 'Meet me at the oak tree,

midday. Say you will.'

Jenny turned to catch up with her father.

'I'll be there,' she heard Alan call after her.

***

William made his way to the vestry to meet Father Joseph. He stood at the window while he waited and shuddered when his gaze fell upon the noose hanging from the oak.

'William …' Father Joseph walked to him, reached out and rested his hands on his shoulders. '… you look more worried than usual. What is it?'

'The noose; it's an abomination. I remember people would sit at tables under the oak, laugh, children playing at their feet. Look at what he's done now. Will his greed and savagery never end?' he said. He turned back to Joseph. 'What news from the King?'

'He is dismayed at this new tax Sir Leonard, your father, has wrought on his people. More importantly, he has heard rumours Sir Leonard is planning to get his hands on the Duchy of Bamburgh.'

'What?' William exclaimed. 'I knew there was something afoot. He's added a number of men to his personal guard. He told me he was readying the guard to collect the tax. The sly dog set the tax up with two prongs to its purpose: one to wreak more pain on the villagers, and one to get us off the scent of Bamburgh.'

'Duke Bebbanburg is on his death bed. With no

heirs, there is no clear successor. It should be the King's prerogative to appoint the next Duke. Sir Leonard knows this but plans to walk into the castle and simply wait 'til the duke dies, then declare the castle and Dukedom his own. The King has already dispatched his men to cut off Sir Leonard at Alnwick and sent messages to Cuthbert in Scotland to await further orders at Berwick-upon-Tweed. Cuthbert will be ordered to strike from the north if Sir Leonard isn't stopped at Alnwick.'

Father Joseph paused to allow William time to take in the news before he asked, 'Will you go ahead with your plans, William?'

William turned to the window and saw Alan with Jenny and Irene. He thought of his childhood and the happy times he'd spent with Jenny and her father, and Alan, who he thought of as his best friend, Jenny, the only girl he ever wanted to marry. He and Alan stayed close and kept their friendship from Hastings; they worked together to keep families in the village safe. This tax was different. It was designed by his father to crush Jim, to set him up and hang him with as many of Jim's friends as he could find. William could stand by no longer. He had to act.

'Yes,' he said, turning to Joseph. 'The King will look kindly upon me if the best we do is weaken him. Should Sir Leonard die, as is my plan, the King will be thankful he did not have to raise arms against his people. I must go, Father.'

'Be careful, William. I will get a message to you if I hear more news.' Father Joseph made the sign of the cross as he watched William stride from his sight.

Joseph turned to the window. He watched Jenny and Irene pick their way over the rocks to follow their father home. He saw William reach the causeway – he didn't pause to acknowledge Alan, but Joseph saw William give a slight nod, then Alan turned and nimbly hopped across the rocks. At the mainland, Alan ran and quickly disappeared into the village streets.

***

Jenny liked Alan; he made her laugh. Irene teased her about Alan's attention, but she shrugged her sister's ideas off as childhood fancy. She didn't love Alan and certainly had no intention of marrying him as her sister's constant prodding suggested. Jenny hid deep her affection for one man; she yearned to see in him the kindness, gentleness, and adoration he had once showed in her presence. She held tight to her secret wish he would find his way back to her.

Jenny stopped, surprised to see Alan standing at the oak tree with several other young men. She had expected him to be alone.

'Alan Curry, don't tell me they've persuaded you to go hunting,' Jenny announced her arrival. 'You go green gutting the fish.'

There were a few guffaws from the group.

'She knows you too well, Al,' one of them said.

'Get away with you. I'll have a pint of ale from you when we get back,' Alan said, laughing and pointing to the Three Horses Inn. He took Jenny by the elbow and moved them away from the men now back-slapping the youngest of them, Dick; it was likely he'd be buying a barrel of ale.

'You're right, Jenny; we are going hunting, a favour for the young Lord Hastings,' Alan said.

'Why you be doing that braggart a favour? What you done to get his temper on you?'

'Look, Jenny, he's not what you think.'

'Bah.'

'No. I haven't time to explain. You have to trust me. Help your da, Jenny; watch out for him while I'm gone.'

'What's going on?' Jenny's eyes narrowed. 'You're scaring me, Alan.'

'Just trust me. We'll be gone a few days. Stay watchful. All I can say is Sir Leonard is out for your da. William is trying to stop him doing any more harm.'

'William is trying to stop his father? You must think me a simpleton if you expect me to believe that.'

'Like I said, Jenny, Will isn't what you think.'

'Will. Since when do you call him Will?''

'Jenny, I have to go. I'll explain when I get back. If you're worried, see anything, tell ya ma. She'll help persuade Jim to go to Berwick. Tell him the fish are running in the Tweed, anything, but keep him safe. I have to go, Jenny, trust me.'

Then Alan was off, running to catch up with the others. She watched till he was out of sight, turned and ran home.

'There you are. Come help me put these wet sheets out to dry,' her ma called, but Jenny ran through the scullery to her bed.

Jenny felt her ma's weight on the bed, then her hand on her shoulder. 'What is it, hinny?'

'Alan told me to look after me da,' and she told her ma everything Alan had said.

'So, it's started,' her ma said.

Jenny sat up, 'What? What's started?'

'Ssshht,' Mary put her finger to her lips. 'There's too much to tell, and you'll find out everything soon enough. For now, all ya need to know is Will and Al stayed friends and vowed to keep the village people as safe as they could from Lord Hastings. Will found out Sir Leonard is planning to hang ya da, Al's da, and a couple of other men.'

Jenny let out a cry of shock.

'Hastings wants rid of 'em because he doesn't like the respect they have in the village; he's going to claim they swindled their way out of paying the full amount of tax due,' her ma explained.

'But I can't believe …' Jenny said.

'Hastings is a man driven by evil. Evil men can do anything for no reason us folk will ever understand.'

'But William's just as bad.'

'No, he isn't lass. Will's bore the brunt of his father's brutality, helped temper his excesses over the years.'

'But how …?'

'Enough questions for now. I need to warn our friends. You hang out the sheets for me and I promise I'll tell you everything.' Mary picked up her shawl and threw it about her shoulders. She looked back at Jenny before leaving the house. 'Take care of Irene. I won't be gone long.'

***

William watched his father ride out from Tynemouth Castle with his order of knights. They were in no hurry, proceeding at walking pace. Sir Leonard charged William with instruction to keep pressure on the people throughout his lands so they wouldn't forget he would be collecting taxes upon his return. William had little choice but to stay, knowing his father's spies would have no trouble reporting any absence. He and Al spent many hours setting up their plans. William could only wait and pray his friend would prevail and return safely. He made his peace with God the same day he committed to kill Lord Hastings. Now he prayed the next time he saw his father would be atop a funeral pyre.

***

Alan and the others waited at Cramlington. William said his father would be there by the afternoon to pick up supplies of mead from the monastery. Alan found a good spot for the ambush. His men backtracked and set up several obstacles he felt sure Hastings would put down to mishaps, mishaps aimed to get rid of at least half the knights with Sir Leonard. The delay of a broken cartwheel would keep them busy for a while, as would nails in the horses' hooves. A tree to fall on several knights was a stretch, but they had to try.

Alan raised his hand to alert his men when he heard voices, and horses, approaching. *There he is.* Hastings came into view; he broke into a hearty laugh at a jest from his knights. *What's this?* He watched Lord Hastings draw his horse to a stop. He got off the horse and Alan saw him pulling his tunic aside as he walked towards the bushes where Alan and his companions were hiding. *He's going to water the bushes; I can't believe our luck.* Alan signalled to his men; they each readied their knives.

Lord Hastings coughed and belched his way to a bush, so close to where Alan crouched. He started to relieve himself. Alan leapt up. His hand clamped on Hastings' mouth as the knife in his other hand sliced across Sir Leonard's throat. Alan lowered the body to the underbrush and signalled to his men to leave.

They ran out of the copse and scattered before the knights' realised Sir Leonard was taking a bit too long.

***

Blue and red flags flapped in the breeze, forming a circle near the oak tree. People milled around food and market stalls within the circle, while others ate at tables under the oak and drank the free beer supplied from the Three Horses Inn.

Horns heralded the arrival of the King and his procession moving towards the makeshift platform in the centre of the circle; people bustled to find a good spot to watch the proceedings.

The King stepped onto the platform, raised his hand, and people fell silent. 'Today I stand before you to present the new Dukedom of Northumbria, which brings together the Dukedoms of Tynemouth and Bamburgh.'

The people cheered.

The King beckoned to William, then handed him a scroll, 'This is the King's decree, Duke William Hastings of Northumbria.'

William bowed to the King, then stood and waved at his people. He smiled to himself; *there will be more celebration tomorrow when I introduce Earl Alan Curry of Hartley and James Dodd, Sheriff of Northumbria.*

William's gaze fell upon Jenny. His smile broadened

as he dipped his head to her. Jenny felt the heat rise at her neck; she demurely lowered her head but kept her eyes fixed on his.

The celebrations continued well into the evening; paper lanterns now swung from branches of the oak, casting colourful lights across the throng. Father Joseph sat on a mound on the cliff of St Mary's Island, smiling, watching. He spotted a young woman make her way across the rocks below.

Jenny found herself at Collie Well. She looked back at the silhouettes of people dancing and listened to the music of sea shanties float across the bay. *Did she dare?* She turned and looked into the well and started to chant:

'Agnes sweet, and Agnes fair …'

'Such a sweet song.'

She startled at the voice.

'M'Lord,' she said when she saw it was William.

'The tide will be coming in soon. I thought I'd rescue the maiden and return her safely to shore.'

'Thank you, Lord Hastings, but I don't think I need rescuing.'

'Maybe not, but maybe I do.'

'You? Forgive me, M'Lord, but look at the people celebrating your honour.'

He nodded. 'Yes, just my point. I'm drowning in the hands of many; I yearn the arms of one.'

'Lord Hastings …' she began.

'Please, I do have a name,' he said. 'You never called me Lord when we were young.'

'Well, William …'

He cut her off, 'No, the name only you got away with calling me.'

For the first time since he arrived, she looked into his face, such a handsome face, searching his eyes, his smiling eyes.

'I never forgot my promise, Jenny,' he said. 'You were always the girl for me.'

'You have a strange way of showing it, Billy.' She let a smile form on her lips.

'I intend to keep my promise. Will you keep yours?' he asked.

'It depends,' she said, teasing him now.

'Ah. And, hmm, depends on what?'

'Your lips know,' she said. He took her face in his hands and gave her a light kiss.

'Yes, that's a good start,' she said.

William guided her to the causeway before they turned and, arm in arm, walked back to the mainland.

Father Joseph rubbed his hands together and smiled. He stood to make his way back to the chantry, stopping for a moment to look up at the stars. 'Well done, St Agnes, well done.'

Where's my Dinner?

Lunch

Eight mems went to lunch
Went to lunch at Bristo's
One mem ate a wonky prawn…
Now he's fish bait in the meadow

Seven mems went to lunch
Went to lunch at Chookie's
One mem ate a rotten egg…
Now she's laying in the meadow

Six mems went to lunch
Went to lunch at Frenchie's
One mem ate an iffy frog…
Now he's croaking in the meadow

Five mems thought of lunch
They thought and thought and thought
A wonky prawn…
A rotten egg…
An iffy frog…
Sent mems to the meadow

76

Five mems went to lunch
Went to lunch, a picnic
They packed their plates and called it brunch…
And ate it in the meadow

Kooljerrenup Conservation Reserve

Molly in the Park

(picture supplied by B & A Plowman)

Picture of a Dog

The police told her to stay away from the case; too sensitive, they said. But she knew; there was one man the facts pointed to, one man committing the crimes, one man who lived near, one man, who, if she blew this, would come after her.

Her editor and mentor, Jeff, didn't like the investigative piece she'd submitted yesterday. He agreed with the police, said he thought the evidence flimsy, although he did think she was onto something. He didn't need more material for the Saturday and Sunday editions and gave Sarah the weekend to provide credible evidence to support her conclusion.

'Sarah, as the piece stands now, it's, at best, interesting supposition, at worst no more than gossipy drivel,' he said. 'I don't need to tell you, you're one of my best reporters – go find the detail.'

He called after her as she opened his office door to leave, 'If you can't deliver by Monday, drop it.'

Sarah knew Jeff was right but reacted to his direction as a put-down. His words were like a laser, searing through to her core, releasing the secret she had kept hidden deep within all these years.

The laptop screen mirrored her cupped face, right

index finger flicking the touchpad scrolling through her research. *I know the key is here. I will find it, then they'll have to believe me.* It was past midnight, early morning Sunday, but there was no way she could stop to sleep. Persistent fluttering in her stomach pushed her on; anxiety would not overwhelm her. Just one word, a phrase might spark insight, point to irrefutable evidence the police would believe.

Her glance occasionally wandered to papers, constantly moving under her fidgeting left hand, strewn across the kitchen table. Her gaze snapped back to a picture. *There. Yes! Why hadn't she noticed it before?*

Sarah's right hand shot to her mouth to stifle a gasp as she heard banging on the front door. *What the…?* There it was again, more insistent, louder.

'Who's there?' her voice a whisper. She leaned against the door as if she could smell, and touch, the person on the other side.

'I know it's late, sorry. I … I need to speak to you … need your help. Please, love, open the door.'

'Oh, you gave me such a scare,' she said as she opened the door. 'Is everything all right? Are you …?'

Fred leaned against the doorjamb, and Sarah stifled a scream. The blood, so much blood. She reached out to support her father as he fell to his knees.

She balanced him, as best she could, against the wall, 'Wait, I need my phone. Hold on, hold on. I need to call for help. I'll be right back.'

She returned, mobile held to her ear, giving her address. She used a towel she'd grabbed from the kitchen to wipe away blood from his face; blood, she realised that was from his hands. She saw his shirt soaked in blood and instinctively put the towel at a point darker and more sodden, pushing to apply pressure to what seemed the source of the bleeding.

Fred tried to speak, his voice a whisper now. She couldn't hear him. *Get closer.* Sarah swallowed hard to stop a rising wave of nausea. She was trapped in the need-to-know space yet begging for the ambulance to arrive, for someone else to be here. *So much blood.* She leant forward, watching his eyes, then turned her head, her ear to his mouth.

She heard the ambulance siren drawing ever closer. Straining to hear Fred, Sarah's senses were jolted by his grating intake of breath before he said, 'He knows I saw him running away. I told him I wouldn't tell,' Fred rasped and began a racking cough.

'Hold on. Please, hold on. You can tell the police. The ambulance is nearly here – they'll call them.'

Fred grabbed her blouse, pleading eyes bore into her, 'No time, he did this to me. He knows you're watching him. Get away, Sarah. Get aw…' Fred gave a long sigh as he slipped into unconsciousness.

'Make way, ma'am, paramedics.'

Sarah scrambled to her feet, staring at the scene

unfolding in front of her. *He knows. No, God, no! God, help me.* The shock threw her back to the pain her five-year-old mind and body suffered from being tormented with bruising nips along her arms, smacked across her back and legs with a leather strap and threatened with more of the same if she told; then locked in a dark cupboard, under the stairs, in her own home. Her father found her screaming, curled up in a corner with her little arms held tight across her head. He didn't know what to do. In his panic at finding his beautiful little girl in such a state, trying to hold her, calm her, he slapped her face to break her descent into hysteria.

Sarah's slow recovery from the trauma only improved after her twelve-year-old brother, Tom, was sent to a special school. Over time, Sarah's psyche built a fragile internal mechanism she learned to use to calm her anxiety and stay in control. Sarah and Tom were kept apart until her twenty-fifth birthday, one short year ago. He moved to be near his mother and father so his young daughter could get to know and spend more time with her grandparents. Sarah kept her distance. The rare occasion they were in close proximity, her father stood by her side.

Sarah snapped out of her memories as she felt hands on her shoulders, gently turning her, steering her towards the kitchen, down onto the chair she left only minutes ago.

'I'll get the kettle on. I've been told a strong cup of tea works wonders at times like these.'

Sarah sat bolt upright. *That voice. His voice.*

She watched his back as he filled the kettle. He turned and saw her watching him.

He smiled. 'Gayle woke me up when she saw the ambulance outside; she'll be here in a minute.' He walked back to the table, stood in front of her, then lowered his face, still smiling, to look into her eyes. 'So, now you need to tell me what father said.'

'Nothing,' she stammered. 'He said nothing. He couldn't breathe, he … he coughed. Nothing …'

'Why don't I believe you?'

Sarah shook her head. 'I don't know,' was all she could think to say. Inside, she was screaming, her heart beating so fast she felt faint. She started to shake.

'Get that cup of tea ready, Tom,' Gayle said, running into the kitchen and kneeling beside Sarah. 'C'mon, Sarah, it's the shock. The adrenaline makes you shake.' Tom handed the cup to Gayle. 'Here, drink this. It does help,' Gayle said, lifting the tea to Sarah's lips.

'Let me look after her. You go and see to Chrissie,' Tom said, reaching to take the cup of tea.

'Give me a minute. I told Chrissie to stay in bed.'

'One of us should be with her. I'll go then,' he said.

Sarah saw a look of concern wash over Gayle's face.

'No,' she said, a little too quickly. 'You're right. You

need to stay here in case they want to ask you both about your father.' Gayle looked at Sarah, stared at her a long moment. 'The paramedics are here; they told me the police are on the way. It's okay, you will be okay,' she said as she left.

Sarah nodded slowly. Did Gayle know? *Is she telling me she knows?* Sarah looked back to Tom, who was leaning over the table, scanning her documents. He picked up the photograph Sarah had noticed moments before Fred started banging on her front door.

He held up the picture of a dog near the local park. 'Did father give you this, or did you snap it?' he asked.

'I took it. I like Molly; she's a groodle, a beautiful dog.' Sarah felt herself start to shake again, the screaming in her brain getting louder – or was she really screaming.

'But there is something else in the picture. Can't you see it, Sarah? Tell me what you see.'

She felt his breath hot on her face. His lips brushed her cheek as he spoke. 'You're hardly breathing, Sarah. Let me help you breathe.'

She grabbed his left arm as he put his hand over her

mouth, his fingers pushing into her cheekbones. His other hand fastened around her neck and squeezed.

Sarah tried to scream for real. The paramedics were at the front door. Gayle might still be there. She squirmed and kicked but his body weight was on her now, pinning her to the chair. Her vision blurred. Her lungs strained for air. She was back in the cupboard. *Dad, help me. The pain. Help me. Stop him …*

His bodyweight pushed her to the floor, the jolt of her landing loosening his hold. She was pushing him off, gulping for air, kicking and pushing him away.

Strong hands grabbed her, and she froze, momentarily stunned. Her vision cleared. Sarah looked at a familiar face, but couldn't quite place where she'd seen this man.

'D.C.I. Rushton. You're safe now,' he said.

She looked past him and saw Gayle holding a long, thick-bladed kitchen knife smeared with blood. Sarah's eyes followed Gayle's stare to Tom lying, still, on the floor.

Gayle said, 'I caught him, more than once, watching Chrissie take a shower. His face …' Gayle's face twisted into a look of disgust. 'I didn't know he was the one hurting the little girls. I didn't know. I saw that photo yesterday on your kitchen table …' She pointed to the one now on the floor next to Tom. 'I knew it was him in the background. He's in the background of another one too, on the edge of the bushes where they found the girl who was raped.'

'Put the knife ...' the Detective said, but Gayle cut him off. 'He had to be stopped. He knew Fred was with you that day because Fred talked about how long it took you to get the dog to stay still when you were in the park. We heard Tom come in; we weren't sure if he overheard me telling your father about the photograph.'

Gayle looked up at Sarah. 'I needed to stay with Chrissie last night. I couldn't leave her alone with him to go to the police. I'm sorry. I'm so sorry. I had to protect my daughter. I'm so sorry, I'm so sorry ...' She dropped the knife and started to sob.

Time to Rest

Gone Fishing

Stumped

She wheels and deals to get time away
Camping with friends too much a need
For time off next week she'll study today
Exam tomorrow then she is freed

Camping with friends too much a need
Dad not so keen after meeting young Jim
Exam tomorrow then she is freed
You're not going anywhere 'till I have words with him

Dad not so keen after meeting young Jim
I have something he can help me do
You're not going anywhere till I have words with him
We'll chat while we paint the room blue

I have something he can help me do
For time off next week she'll study today
They'll be in Broome to paint the room blue
She wheels and deals to get time away

How are you going with the riddle on page 19?

Here it is again in the style of a pantoum.

Clue:

You will see it in sporting arenas all over the world

What Am I?

Forever at the heart of the four crowns
I was there at the beginning
My portcullis strikes for your renown
Wielded through the ages, losing and winning

I was there at the beginning
I shall be there at the end
Wielded through the ages losing and winning
Against a foe attack and defend

I shall be there at the end
My orb of power unleashed and hurled
Against a foe attack and defend
I am the centre of your world

My orb of power unleashed and hurled
My portcullis strikes for your renown
I am the centre of your world
Forever at the heart of the four crowns

... Behind the Green Door?

The Room

Doors pushed open wide
cold wind made entry quick
chilling occupants within
turning heads eyes look grim

Your gaze rests on
expressionless faces
a greeting so profound
not a murmur not a sound

A rustle here a sniff there
stolen glance from bent head
silence order of the day
niceties gone astray

Air hangs thick
frayed temper irritation
naught can surpass the gloom
of a dank cold waiting room

Three Chocolate Mousse: A Just Dessert.

Just Desserts

Co-Authors: Sandra Smiles, Robyn Clemen
& John Kevan

Characters of the Play

JACK WILSON   SYLVIA SMYTHE   PENNY POCOCK

WAITRESS   NARRATOR (The Voice)

The play takes place in the subdued lighting of a restaurant.

TIME: *The present.*

SCENE: *A few tables, one at centre stage with three place settings. The waitress is hovering. Light dinner music is playing.*

ACT ONE: APERITIF

NARRATOR: It's a slow night at the French restaurant, Coffin la Finale, a good night for the new waitress to reveal her skills, which shouldn't be hard with only three guests booked.

(Waitress looks about, glowers)

Ah, our first guest, Sylvia, has arrived; a tad overdressed for this drab establishment if you ask me.

WAITRESS: No one is asking you. Let's get this play started …

The waitress follows our guest, Sylvia, to the table. Sylvia is nervous, plays with her telephone and puts her coat/jacket on the back of the chair. She pats her hair, straights her low-cut dress, fidgets.

The waitress gives Sylvia a menu and takes the bottle of wine Sylvia brought with her.

NARRATOR: Heee-re's Jack.

Jack enters left of stage and watches Sylvia for a moment. He fusses a little with his clothes.

Jack isn't making sure he looks good, he's wondering whether he'll get away without revealing too much of the truth, the dirty, sleazy, backstabbing truth

JACK: Shut up. I'm not hiding anything.

NARRATOR: Then what's with the bow on the wine – bit over the top, isn't it?

SYLVIA: (*standing to greet him*) Jack.

JACK: (*smiling*) Wow – you're much prettier than your picture.

SYLVIA: (*awkward, cool*) … and you're taller than I expected

They sit. Waitress brings Sylvia's bottle of wine in an ice bucket and a couple of glasses.

SYLVIA: Hope you don't mind? I brought a bottle of wine.

WAITRESS: (*smiling and pouring the wine*)

Chateau du Morte; It's a beautiful wine with a light, but full flavoured body. It's a popular choice with our signature dish, La Fin d'Tartare.

JACK: Good lord! That's my favourite wine – you must be a mind reader.

SYLVIA: And I see you brought the same – are you aiming to ply my me with alcohol, Jack?

Jack gives his bottle to the waitress and picks up the menu.

JACK: Shall I order us some oysters? Something tells me you'd enjoy them.

SYLVIA: Yes, I do like oysters – good guess … or perhaps someone told you?

NARRATOR: I wonder what he has on his mind?

Jack calls over the waitress.

JACK: We'll both have the oysters natural please. *(turns to Sylvia)* So tell me about yourself. You said you live south of the river, I guess Mandurah? – Do you work there? Have you ever been married? Any kids?

SYLVIA: *(Gives a laugh)* Let's see if I can answer in order. Yes, Mandurah. No I don't work there but I am a teacher. Never married. No kids. One sibling, a sister who has been dead over a year now … And yourself?

JACK: I'm a medical researcher at UWA, not married, no kids.

Waitress brings the oysters.

WAITRESS: Are you ready to order your main course, or do you need a little more time?

JACK: Sylvia, are you ready to order?

(she nods)

We'll order now. I'll have the fish, thank you.

SYLVIA: Veal medallions, medium, thanks

Both begin to eat their oysters and flirt, while love music plays

SYLVIA: My sister was a medical researcher at UWA as well … but you already know that, don't you? Right back when I first contacted you on the dating site – you knew I was Bridget's sister. *(slight pause, accusatory tone)* Didn't you?

Music goes awry

NARRATOR: Told you he's hiding something. Get yourself out of that one, Jack.

JACK: *(holds up his hands in mock surrender)*

Guilty as charged. I knew it was too much of a coincidence for you not to know Bridget and I were not only in a relationship, but co-workers as well. *(tilts his head slightly, questioning look)* So why did you meet up with me here?

SYLVIA: I wanted to meet the man who murdered my sister.

Music booms

NARRATOR: Even I didn't see that one coming. But I can see our third guest, Penny, has arrived. Ha, they haven't seen her yet; Hmmm, nice swishy hips …

Music

Jack and Sylvia look around – where's the music coming from?

ACT TWO: MAIN COURSE

NARRATOR: Penny is a lady with a lot on her mind. And she is mightily pissed off they've eaten the oysters

Penny gives a bottle of wine to the waitress before she reaches Jack and Sylvia.

Waitress returns, fills Penny's wine glass and removes dirty plates. Returns and hovers, listening to their conversation, waiting for Penny's order

PENNY: Well – looks like you two are hitting it off OK – I thought you might. I see you started dinner without me, Jack.

JACK: (*slight hesitation*) Hello, Penny. Good to see you. Umm, allow me to introduce you to Sylvia, Bridget's sister.

PENNY: Yes, we have met. In fact, it was my suggestion we meet up tonight – the three of us have some matters to discuss, don't we, Sylvia?

(Penny and Sylvia clasp hands affectionately)

So nice to see you again. What happened to Bridget was so awful. I do hope you're coping with your tragic loss.

Jack gives a questioning look at Sylvia, Penny turns to Jack

PENNY: Don't look so surprised, Jack. Sylvia and I met when Bridget and I did the field visit to Rottnest. Oh dear, you can't have forgotten I was your Admin Research Assistant. We worked so close together at UWA.

(Jack glowers at Penny. Penny laughs)

Only teasing ... Have you discussed the agreed changes to the patent

	application for the biometrics yet?
SYLVIA:	(*nasty, spitting voice*)
	Patent? What bloody patent? Neither you nor Bridget mentioned a patent to me?
	(*hard look at Jack and Penny*)
	Music – 'Jaws'
PENNY:	Ooops… (*slight pause*) It's my guess you both forgot to mention to each other I was joining you for dinner? Which reminds me … (*to the waitress*) … Coq-au-Vin, thanks
	Waitress leaves.
SYLVIA:	No, Jack didn't mention he knew that. (*pause*) I invited you here to support me.
JACK:	I suggested you come later, Penny …
SYLVIA:	(*with emphasis*) So why is she here? Why the both of us, Jack?
NARRATOR:	Good question
SYLVIA:	And what's all this about a patent for the work you and Bridget were

doing? Please … explain.

NARRATOR: Yes, please explain, Jack. This is getting juicy

JACK: (*looking about at the voice, frustrated*)

It isn't juicy …

(*looks back to Sylvia*)

Look, it's very simple: we … me and Bridget … put an application together, but it's on hold, pending. You see (*glances at Penny*), well … Penny pointed out she should have been named on the patent. We were in the process of updating the application when Bridget, well … when Bridget died unexpectedly.

SYLVIA: So, you invited me here because, as Bridget's only relative, I inherit her part of the patent.

JACK: Well, yes, but Bridget agreed to add Penny, three of us. Each with one-third interest.

NARRATOR: I can hear a ticking noise … ah, it's Sylvia, calculating

Waitress returns, serves the main meals.

Then hovers listening to their conversation

SYLVIA: What's the patent worth? Is there a monetary value or purely academic?

JACK: Both actually. The academic credit is likely to be life-long recognition, and yes; the patent does have an estimated value … depending on whether we sell it outright or take a cut of the income of sale of the final product …

SYLVIA: Well spit it out. How much?

JACK: Your cut of the sale is likely to be $6 million. Our advice is money from part of the sale of product won't be realised for some time, because of production and distribution costs. Sales could be as little as $600,000 or much more. It's … well … it's a big risk. Selling the patent will give us certainty.

SYLVIA: You said the patent sale has been delayed so Penny could be added as a beneficiary?

(Jack nods).

So – the total value is $18 million?

(*Jack nods*)

… and without any change, as Bridget's beneficiary, I will get $9 million? If Penny is added that will drop to $6 million.

Music: Money

NARRATOR: Aha! By George, she's got it. What's next …?

PENNY: (*looking around at the voice*)

Shut up and we'll all know

Jack and Penny glance at each other and nod

SYLVIA: What's left to be done to get the amended patent through?

Jack hurriedly pulls out a folded document from his jacket pocket and spreads out in front of Sylvia

JACK: Penny and I have already signed. You just need to sign here, and here …

(*Jack points to the document*)

Sylvia puts on glasses and studies the document carefully.

Jack and Penny watch Sylvia reading the document

SYLVIA:	Surely if Bridget wanted to recognise Penny's work, she would have agreed to her name being in the original patent application. (*Sylvia turns to Penny*). When we were together, you had only just been appointed as an assistant to Jack and Bridget.
PENNY:	How I started is irrelevant. I did a significant amount of work. I deserve to be recognised.
JACK	(*angrily*) Look, I did all the bloody scientific work. Bridget nudged me on a couple of targets, but the whole project was my baby. (*looking at both Penny and Sylvia*) Neither one of you is entitled to anything.
NARRATOR:	Eeeeeow. Testy … Testy …
ALL:	SHUT UP!
SYLVIA:	So why did you sign the papers? No. I refuse to sign. (*Pushes documents into the middle of table, throws her glasses on top*)

I understand the amount of work Bridget put in *(she stops and nods)*

Ahhh, and it was *her* idea … wasn't it, Jack? The real issue is neither of you have a right to have your names on the patent.

(Sylvia raises her voice)

Is that why you killed her? To get your hands on the patent and the money.

(Sylvia turns on Penny)

Or was it you?

Sylvia snatches the papers and puts them in her bag

PENNY: Don't be ridiculous. Kill Bridget … ha! I just wanted my fair share.

JACK: Stop it. Stop it. We need to calm down. We need to be reasonable and sort this out …

SYLVIA: *(rising to her feet, fiercely hisses)*

Don't you bloody well tell me to calm down.

Waitress has been hovering and moves to the table to clear plates.

Sylvia storms off to the powder room.

PENNY: You bloody fool. "Leave it to me. I'll handle it," you said. I told you Sylvia is a money-grabbing bitch. Bridget told me Sylvia poisoned their mother to get her hands on the family money. I haven't told you, but I saw her in the university grounds the day before Bridget died. (*pause*) And, of course, when do you intend to tell her you need the money to pay back what you stole from the research fund, not to mention your gambling debts?

JACK: Don't you dare threaten me, and you're grasping at straws if you think anyone will believe you now about seeing Sylvia the day before Bridget died. What do you think you're up to …?

PENNY: Calm down, Jack. I thought Sylvia was visiting you, and you do have gambling debts … Anyway, why are we fighting over this? We're in this together — we're getting married when this is sorted out, remember? Or has Sylvia changed your mind already? I see the way you're fawning over her and I don't like it. (*Voice rising, almost hysterical*) Don't you even think of throwing me over for her; I swear, I'll kill the both of you if you even think of it.

Sylvia has returned and heard them arguing.

She sits, while Jack and Penny are now glaring at each other

SYLVIA: Oh my god. (*accusatory*) You two *are* in this together. You had an affair … behind Bridget's back (*cynical laugh*), you cooked all this up. You were both in on her murder … you murdering bastards!

Music – 'Midsomer'

ACT THREE: DESSERT

NARRATOR: Jack's chances with Sylvia are out the window. His worried look is because he's wishing he had gone with something cheaper than oysters.

(*Jack glowers at the voice*)

Penny can see her plans of marrying Jack being flushed down the toilet

(*Penny gives the voice a finger*)

They are all wondering which bank has a branch in the Cayman Islands,

(*they all shake their heads*)

well that's what I'd be doing right now. We are about to find out who killed Bridget – but there again, ha who cares, it's all about who gets the money now.

SYLVIA:		Jack, what the hell is going on here?

The waitress returns to take their dessert orders. They all use the distraction to gather their thoughts – they gaze at their menus.

Penny stretches forward and with a deft hand movement appears to put something into Jack and Sylvia's wine. Jack orders

JACK:		The 'Three Chocolate Mousse' sounds nice. What do you think?

(*Penny and Sylvia both nod*)

(Jack *to the waitress*)

Three mousse, thanks.

NARRATOR:	C'mon, Jack, back to the question. What the hell is going on? You've lost me.

PENNY: Why're you asking, Jack? He left for America in the early morning. Bridget was seen by co-workers. Perhaps you saw her too?

SYLVIA: What on earth do you mean? I was in Mandurah. Come to think of it, where were you, Penny? And Jack didn't get on the plane, did you? All Jetstar flights were grounded for 24 hours because of a computer glitch.

PENNY: *(Penny turns on Sylvia)*

You're only concerned about the money. You're not happy with six million. Probably not with half either. You should watch yourself, Jack, she's coming for you. The greedy bitch wants the lot.

SYLVIA: And you don't? Why are you chasing Jack? Think you can get him to put a ring on your finger? What then, pop him off …? I know who the real greedy bitch is …

NARRATOR: Ahhh, there it is – each of them wants the lot. Hmm. Maybe I can get my finger in the pie …

They all give the voice the finger.

Jack and Sylvia were about to take a sip of wine but the waitress returns and sets about placing their orders on the table.

They put their wine glasses down.

Jack is agitated, fiddling with the wine glass.

The others reach for and raise their glass and promptly put them down without taking a drink.

JACK: (*angrily*) Will you all shut up! That means you too (*looking about at the voice*). This isn't easy but the two of you (*pointing to Sylvia and Penny*) arguing isn't helping. We can all come out of this significantly better off.

(*he turns to look at Sylvia*)

No, I didn't go to America. When the flights were cancelled, I … I went to the casino, lost a lot of money …

PENNY: Including the research dollars …

JACK: Shut up, Penny. The point is I wasn't at the university, I didn't kill Bridget, I didn't kill anyone.

NARRATOR: Here it is, the dirty, sleazy secret …

JACK: (*to the voice*) What's so secret or sleazy about hearing Bridget had a heart attack? Now will you shut up and let me get through my lines.

NARRATOR: Have a drink, it's going off …

JACK: (*shaking his head*) My reputation is on the line. I can't sink any deeper. The one thing I know is it wasn't me that caused Bridget to disappear. If she was murdered, it was someone else, who did it, not me. You both seem to think it was murder. Why …?

Oh hang on, don't tell me, you're both in on it together …

All look around and raise their hands, warning the voice to keep quiet

SYLVIA: Don't be stupid. I came here to confront you. Why would I step into the limelight if I killed her?

PENNY: But you know he is partly right – we have some history, Sylvia. We were together a while.

SYLVIA: (*bows her head - speaks defensively*)

That was a silly mistake – I was going through an experimental stage of my life.

PENNY: You didn't say that at the time. You'd better watch out, Jack – this lady doesn't seem to care who's in her bed as long as she gets what she wants.

SYLVIA: (*looks up with a new thought on her mind, points her finger at Penny*)

Bridget and Jack were talking about marrying and you killed her because you wanted him for yourself.

JACK: (*Jack leers*). Ladies, ladies. (*Opens his arms wide*). You can both have me. We're all after the same thing – why don't we join forces – it could be a very profitable and … ummm, satisfying relationship if we are a team.

NARRATOR: See, told you – sleaze. Can't see you keeping both ladies happy, Jack.

Penny curls her lip. Sylvia is aghast. They both glare at

Jack who holds up his hands in mock surrender then picks up his glass.

Sylvia picks up her glass and Penny does the same.

JACK: Let's sit back, enjoy the wine, while one of you 'fesses up, or I will drop you both in it.

Jack and Sylvia take a large drink of their wine.

Penny gazes into her glass and smiles

NARRATOR: Eventually, they drink the wine. Well, is it as good as the waitress told us?

Jack and Penny put their wine glasses down

PENNY: (*smiling at Jack*) Well, Jack, you're certainly acting high and mighty now. I checked with the lawyers, by the way, just in case. I thought Sylvia would be unlikely to sign. The lawyers said it might take a short court case to verify her, let's say, approval. All we need is evidence that suggests she was in agreement, like meeting us for dinner to sign the application. My inclusion on the patent will happen.

JACK: What are you trying to say?

PENNY: I also checked I can verify our relationship. You see I have photographs of us together, the ring you bought for me …

Penny raises her glass but doesn't drink.

Sylvia sips her wine, watching Jack and Penny argue.

JACK: I haven't bought a bloody ring …

PENNY: Oh, don't you remember, darling? It matches my engagement ring.

                    (Penny waggles her ring finger.

                    Jack splutters, Sylvia's shoulders slightly drop and she lowers her head)

        I realised early on you and Bridget were onto something. You both kept me at arms-length so I had to work something out – too much money for you both – a third share wasn't that much to worry about. But then I thought why not all of it?

Sylvia drinks more wine

JACK: No, you can't be, you couldn't …

NARRATOR: Stop blubbering, Jack. Surely your lines are better than that.

PENNY: Oh, but I did, Jack. All of it. And now Sylvia has finished her wine, it won't be long before the pain in her heart kills her, then we can be together … for a while at least.

They both look at Sylvia who has grasped her throat.

Sylvia's face contorts, as she grabs her chest

JACK: My god, what is happening?

(Gasps, clutches his chest)

The wine … you, you poisoned the wine …

NARRATOR: No wonder no-one wanted to drink it

PENNY: Yes, you two-faced bastard. Did you really think I would let you get away with it? I murdered Bridget for you. The next thing I know, you're trying it on with Bridget's sister – no way!

Jack slumps dead onto the table.

PENNY: This deserves a toast.

Penny picks up her glass goes to drink, stops, smiles, waggles her finger and shakes her head

PENNY: Waitress! Can you bring me the wine I brought with me please?

Waitress arrives with the wine. Looks at the two bodies and then looks askance at Penny. Penny shrugs as she stands and toasts Sylvia and Jack.

PENNY: They never could hold their drink — (*aside to the waitress*) maybe it was the oysters.

She gulps another mouthful, then she gasps and clutches her chest.

NARRATOR: Oh, oh, but wait, there's more …

The waitress pulls off her wig and glasses.

Penny slumps back into her chair looking up.

PENNY: Bridget, it's you... but how?

BRIDGET: (*formerly the waitress*). Neither you, nor Jack, hung around long enough to find out: the ambo's managed to revive me on the way to the hospital. I'd collapsed with severe stomach spasms - it wasn't a heart attack.

I left hospital the next day and

went interstate for a few months while I planned my revenge.

PENNY: *(gasping)* You'll never get away with this.

BRIDGET: Oh, contraire. I'll lay low for a while and reappear in a few weeks – no one will suspect me for any of this.

Bridget retrieves the documents from Sylvia's bag.

BRIDGET: What a cushy life I'll have with $18 million at my disposal. Ta. Ta.

Penny slumps dead on the table. Bridget leaves.

NARRATOR: Noice...! No waitress, dead bodies everywhere, chefs not gonna be happy there's no-one to pay the bill. Oh, No. No. No. No. Not me, I'm outta here …!

Drabbles

A drabble is a story with precisely 100 words (not including the title). It is one of the many forms of the Flash-Fiction genre which generally has word limits as low as 6 up to 1,000. A dribble, for instance, is a story of 50 words.

I admit I find them quite a challenge and I have included three as examples of my efforts.

Spike

I shuffled towards the theatre doors. A group was making headway through the throng so I followed, and continued to follow once outside, my curiosity piqued by their excited chatter and momentum towards their goal.

We turned down the alley, arriving at the stage door as it opened and we were led into a dim sitting room where our host sat, sipping a cup of tea.

Looking tired, he gave us a weary smile. Make-up was gone, no lights heightened his aura. Yet we stood in awe of this ordinary man possessed with a sublime ability to make people laugh.

Some Things Never Change

The jingle echoed in the distance. Our eyes wide in excited anticipation. Brother bounced in childish delight. A smile spread across my measles spotted face. Mum appeared with a sixpence before the music stopped at our front door.

Brother handed over the sixpence, Mr Whippy safely delivered two cones to five-year-old hands. Glee turned to horror as ten-year-old next door grabbed brother's hands and sucked off the peaks of ice-cream towers. Tears abated as Mum restored order.

Self-isolate today's catch cry. Happy memories awake, a smile spreads across my wrinkled face. Greensleeves heralds the coming! Then Mr Whippy cruises by.

Time Well Spent

The monk bowed. 'Hello, old friend. I will sit with you till dawn.' The candle flame flickered its acknowledgement. It burned brightly at the window, visible for miles around.

Brother Jacob sat on a stool next to a bare oak table, clasped his hands and silently prayed. *Brethren, for many centuries, have guarded souls passing our shore. Father keep steady the hearts of men who follow.*

Dawn broke. The flame flickered, spluttered and died. The monk stood to look beyond where candles had stood for centuries, through the window, to the tapered cylindrical tower of the new St Mary's lighthouse.

Bush Poetry

I do enjoy 'going bush' in the Australian Outback.

The following small selection of poems, written while on the track, offers a peek into odd moments that brought much hilarity to camp and strengthened the bond of lasting friendships.

Tyres

Saturday morning, we answered the call
to get ready if a flattie should befall.
Repair a split-rim tyre the lesson of the day,
'cause in the bush it's our job, come what may.
Roger conducted the demonstration,
our whirring camera caused consternation.
On he proceeded with a hands-on approach
six questioning ladies not easy to coach.
Copious notes taken; each step etched in our brain
confident our memories would let us do it again.

The Gunbarrel Highway
gave us our first naughty tyre
we leapt at the chance to fix it, no hint of ire.
The sterile field created with a worn dusty tarp
sounds of preparation like a tinkling harp.
The tyre attacked by six brains and six pairs of hands
sounding like we'd learnt in six different lands.
One by one we left,
as important points we didn't agree
the beads not broken, only two levers not three.
It was then the fix-it team was borne
as they huffed and puffed to what seemed like dawn.

Tyre taken apart, reassembled with care
then panic set in, the Blue Tongue lost – no air!
Disaster was avoided, all allowed back in camp,
we found young bluey who worked a wonder –
little champ
Tyre back on, four wheels again, now to be tested
The FT Team had beer and were duly rested.

Next morning the tyre was still hard and intact
Stayed that way for the rest of the trip, in fact.

The Fix It Team

With just a moment's notice they will attend
To assist with the thing you need to mend
Their imaginations run riot, ideas drip into pools
of oil, grease and sweat and quite unique tools

'Just what do they fix?' I hear you ask
Well, let me recall the odd little task
A tyre on the Gunbarrel, split-rim were they
bead duly broken, fixed, soon on our way

Out came the wire for the billy at Well One
there was a bit of mumbling but the job got done
Sweaty feet, age and dust they did succumb
Multi-grips applied to boots requiring gum

The battery mount caused a stir and worry
something wedged in, now proceed, no hurry
flags, camera, chair, camp bed
number plate, a boil ... not a worry they said

Our Fix It Team those recalcitrant bits did tether
Surprising really when it all held together

Lost

Not 70 ks from Marla
at the cattle grid turn right
go around the waterhole,
bet they'll be there in plain sight

A voice from the shower
alerted us to their plight
'I put them under the car
for protection overnight!'

Two took off, back down the track
the mercy mission to attend
Some waited with bright idea,
cream-cakes, to befriend

The search began in earnest
cattle grid and waterhole found
two black boots spotted
rescued soon homeward bound.

Twelve

'Isn't this amazing?'
no truer words forsake
a marvel to behold
better than chook or steak

'Oooh, just look at these!'
and the camp viewed in awe
at those not so little buggers
paraded in the raw

'I did ask for thick ones,
but look at what I got!'
Twelve of the fattest sausages
ever squeezed in the bedourie pot

Bush Walk: Newman, Western Australia

Mr Peter's Holiday

The fog descended upon the city. All day it hung heavy in the air, shrouded trees and buildings and swallowed people into its grey cloak. Street noise was muffled, only hinting at the shuffling city life within the fog's damp cocoon. At the end of the long, depressing day, people scurried homeward or found warmth at the hearth of a public house.

Graham Peters closed the door as he stepped into the hallway of his home, where he was greeted by his valet ready to help him remove his heavy, wet overcoat.

'Thank you, Wilson, damnable weather, set for a few days yet I think,' he said.

'Quite, sir,' Wilson replied. 'I sent cook home an hour ago. She complained all day about her chilblains.'

They both raised their eyebrows and shared a smile. Mrs Tucker complained daily about one pain or another, all reliant on the weather of the day.

'She left you supper and asked me to tell you she trusts you will enjoy your holiday.'

Graham nodded. 'Thank you. Is everything set?'

'Yes, sir. I personally made sure your luggage was taken aboard the ship. The house is ready; all you need do is lock the front door as you leave in the morning.'

'I bet Mrs Wilson is looking forward to having you home for a few weeks?'

'Yes, she is. I am not so sure I am looking forward to it though. My list of chores grows daily.'

'Well, you had better be off, Wilson. I can look after myself for a few hours. I'm looking forward to dinner tonight with Miss Everingham at the Palace Grande.'

'Thank you, Mr Peters. I'll have everything back up and running here ready for your return. Enjoy your holiday, sir; well deserved.'

'Good night, Wilson.'

Graham dressed for dinner, poured himself a brandy, and sunk into his soft leather chair. The doorbell rang as he raised the glass to his lips.

'What the devil?' he said, rather testily. He continued muttering to himself as he stood up, placed the glass on the table and strode to open the door.

A young boy, too scantily clad for the weather, raised his arm, holding out an envelope. 'A note from Mr Mason, sir.'

'Thank you,' Graham said as he reached for his wallet. He held up a five-pound note. 'Buy coal and food for your family on your way home.' Graham gave a stern look as he nodded to the boy.

The boy dipped his head in return. 'Yes, sir. Thank you, sir.' He handed over the envelope and ran off.

Graham watched the boy disappear into the fog. '...

but for the grace of God,' he thought.

Graham was orphaned at the age of six. He lay with his mother in a shop doorway, not realising she had died during the night. No one took notice of the six-year-old, who snuck behind a rubbish bin as his mother's body was removed. A carpenter found him. Graham Peters took the boy home, called him Graham after himself and raised him as his son. Graham Peters Senior never married but did set up and grow his own timber business, Peters Timber. He accumulated wealth quickly and gave his son every opportunity, including having him attend Eton. Graham Peters Junior never forgot the pain and hunger of his early years. He, too, was a good businessman and became a well-known and well-regarded philanthropist.

Graham closed the door, returned to his study and retrieved the glass of brandy before sitting back into his armchair. He twirled the envelope in his fingers while he sipped the brandy. He sighed and wondered, *why tonight?*

Graham reflected on his work day, checking off in his mind he had indeed cleared his desk, nothing left undone before his holiday. Then he smiled. Paul was a reliable friend, much more than a business partner. He had been the one to suggest a holiday. He recalled Paul laughing as he said that if he didn't disclose his itinerary, he wouldn't be pestered by associates or bankers chasing his favour.

'What tomfoolery are you up to, Mr Mason?' he thought.

Graham opened the envelope. Unfolding the paper, he noted a hurried scrawl which made him frown. *Most unlike Paul, his writing is always impeccable.* He started as he read:

'Return to the office immediately – explain when you get here, hurry!'

'Good God!' Graham jumped to his feet. He grabbed his coat and ran out of the house into the street. He kept running until he managed to attract the attention of a cabbie.

He calmed once in the hansom cab, his mind fixed on the only reason he could think of to be called with such urgency: one of his ships had gone down. He gave a silent prayer that no lives had been lost. Paul, although a capable businessman, wouldn't want to deal with a disaster like that by himself.

Graham's thoughts went to Emma who, only a few short days ago, had accepted his proposal of marriage.

Her eyes sparkled as she said, 'Oh, Darling, I won't miss you at all while you are away. I shall be too busy with the arrangements for our wedding.'

'Don't get too carried away, and don't let your mother control who gets onto the invitation list,' he replied, knowing full well she would indeed wrest control of the proceedings.

I'll have just enough time to send her a note once I get to the office.

Graham sighed, knowing it unlikely he would be dining with Emma this evening and sad his meticulous plans would come to nought. Emma was always very punctual – a quality he admired and one that she teased him about – he was invariably late! He arranged to be at her home by 7.30; she had laughed and said, 'Then I shall be ready at 8.00.' Tonight, he had intended to arrive at her doorstep at 7.25.

He was jolted from his reverie by a cab passing dangerously close to his, causing a sudden swerve. Raised voices were heard above the clatter of the horses' hooves on the cobbled street. His shoulder painfully bounced against the door of the hansom cab. He heard the two drivers cursing each other, both drunk from whisky consumed to ward off the cold.

Graham used his walking stick to hit the roof of the cab. 'Driver, you there, steady down, steady down man …'

The Cabbie grunted a reply, '… Sir…'

Graham gathered himself. For the remainder of the journey his mind returned to weaving around the message.

The cab stopped. 'Peters Timber, sir,' the cabbie grunted their arrival.

Graham alighted and shuddered as the damp and cold invaded his lungs, moisture quickly forming droplets on his heavy woven overcoat. He hurried toward the large building and the warmth and protection of his office. His footsteps on the newly polished floor echoed in the empty hallway.

He opened his office door, stepping across the threshold in one fluid, oft-repeated, motion. His head snapped back at the same instant he heard a sharp retort. Confused, he became aware of a searing pain in his chest. His hands felt wet, sticky, pulling at his overcoat, vision fading. Graham dropped to his knees, hands pressing his chest, vainly grasping at a wracking pain …

Graham registered a primal mental agony as he saw Paul take Emma into his arms. His final word, a fading whisper, 'Why…?'

Next morning fog still shielded the city like a bride's veil, and people went about their business despite nature's bad mood. At the bustling east wharf, a ship hoisted its sails to catch the morning air as its passengers settled belongings into their cabins or walked the decks. Cabin 103 lay undisturbed.

Paul Mason arrived at the office, prompt at 9am sharp, as always.

'Morning, Mrs Temple. Anything of interest in the newspaper this morning?'

'Good morning, Mr Mason,' she replied. 'Mr Peters and you both got a mention in the society column. It says Mr Graham Peters was taking a well-earned holiday, leaving the daily running of the business in the capable hands of his partner, Mr Paul Mason. It made mention that Mr Peters had not disclosed his intended destination, bet that has everyone talking.'

'Yes, quite,' he replied.

Put Your Shoes On: Shoe Tree, Herron Point, Western Australia

What am I?

A Tennis Racket

Sunset, Onslow Beach, Western Australia.

Birthday Adventure

Mum was antsy all day. Ten years ago, Bof took me on a birthday adventure; he didn't come home. It's my twenty-first birthday tomorrow. The accident happened the day before my eleventh birthday and became the focal point of my life memories. Every year, on this day, they flash by like snippets of the old black and white Buster Keating and Charlie Chaplin movies Bof so loved to watch. Bof, ever-present in my mind, no doubt hers too. My birthday. Bof's death. Inseparable.

Mum wasn't pleased I went with him. She was in the throes of getting everything ready for my party. I was supposed to be tidying my room and putting away my toys, but I knew he would come for me and sat waiting, out of Mum's sight, near the front door.

'Will you go and tidy your room,' my mum shouted from the kitchen.

How does she know I'm here? crossed my mind at the same time I heard a knock at the door.

'I'll get it,' I called.

I jumped as she swished past me to yank the door open. *How'd she get here so quick?*

Hands went to her hips as she snapped, 'I told you, Dad, not today!'

'We won't be long, love. You know it's our tradition. The day before his birthday, I take him for a drive to a mystery place. I promise I'll get him back in plenty of time to do his chores.'

'And you know we have our own tradition through his fathers' family.' She pointed to me, making it clear she was talking about my dad's family. 'Turning eleven is a special birthday for us.'

'I haven't heard anyone making eleven a special birthday,' my grandad said. 'Thirteen, eighteen, twenty-one, maybe ...,' and on he went as only Bof could.

He wouldn't be shut up – if he had something to say, he said it. 'Why use one word when a hundred says it so much better?' his motto. The family called it being a boring old fart. Over time, they, and I, just called him Bof.

I stepped forward to give him a hand and started whining, 'But, Mum, I want to go. I promise I'll clean my room.'

Mum lost her cool. 'Oh, stop it, the pair of you. Back by four, or else.'

I raced out and heard the door slam.

He took me to the museum to see the Chinese clay warriors. His words weaved a magic spell as he told the story of how the first Emperor of China wanted to be buried with a full army to protect him on his journey to the afterlife.

We finished our visit with an ice cream in the cafe, where he gave me my birthday present.

'Thank you, Bof. I'm not going to open it 'til tomorrow.'

'Good idea,' he said.

We were almost home, waiting at the intersection for the traffic lights to change.

'Make sure you do what your mum says,' he said.

The traffic light turned green. Bof edged the car to the centre of the road, prepared to turn right, and everything went black.

I got home several weeks later, welcomed with a delayed party.

'Better do something with these presents,' my dad said.

I ripped into them. My favourite present was a steam engine with extension tracks for my train set. I couldn't bring myself to open the present from Bof. I peeled off the torn, dirty wrapping paper. Grit and grime fell onto the table. I held a small red chest in my hand. It was heavy, and I heard a muffled sound like one piece of metal brushing against another as I placed it on the table. I couldn't open it.

I looked at Mum. She stood with her right arm wrapped around her chest, her left hand at her mouth.

Tears ran down her cheeks.

She turned to Dad. 'I shouldn't have let him go. I should've made him stay and clean his room.'

I went to Mum and gave her a hug. She shook herself and pushed me away.

'It's okay, love – he's telling you he loves you,' Dad said and winked at me.

I didn't hug her much after that. I know she loves me, but she misses Bof. I get it … she thinks the accident was her fault.

Dad and I got around to planning the new layout of the train tracks and spent hours setting it up.

'Put the station there, Dad.'

'Hmm, I think he would really like the station here.'

I nodded. 'Yeah, great choice. Hey, Dad, what about putting the mountain tunnel the first obstacle the train reaches?'

'I think you will like having the train emerge from the mountain tunnel to descend to the station,' he said.

'Wow, yeah. It looks great, Dad.'

I fell asleep watching and listening to the steam engine chugging around our new layout. Choooo, Choo, ssst.

I woke up. I couldn't hear the rhythmic chuffing of my train. Dad must have turned it off when he looked in to say goodnight. I started coughing. My throat … something in my throat. I yelled for Mum. *Can't breathe.*

Hot. Too hot, get the blankets off me. My fists clench, my legs kick … *Mum, help me, Mum …*

'Shh, I'm here. We're both here, sshh, sshh.'

I turned my head to her voice and saw Dad bending, holding a plug. A moment later, the train started. Chooooooooo, Choo, ssst.

I went back to sleep.

The next day my dad rearranged my bedroom and put the train set next to my bed. He used to turn off the train at night, but I turned it back on when I heard the floorboards creak and his bedroom door close.

I overheard my mum and dad talking one evening.

'There's a new Principal at the high school. He rang me today, left a message,' Dad said.

'Will you call him tomorrow to let him know, explain?' Mum asked.

'Yeah.'

With that, I was back at school.

The coolest thing about school was Beth, my girlfriend who I'd met when I was ten. We promised to stay together forever.

The day we both decided to study law, I had taken refuge at her place from Mum's wrath. I hadn't slept well, just lay and watched the steam train, choooo, choo, ssst, its way around the tracks. Then it hit me. I knew what was missing.

I tiptoed around the kitchen and gathered everything I needed. I was so happy with the outcome. I sat back on my heels as the steam train gently pulled away from the station. It gathered speed to cruise through the Parsley Meadows, into the Cinnamon Stick forest, to emerge to descend into the Turmeric Desert before it started to climb the ice capped Plain Flour mountain. The train made its way through the tunnel before descending into the Peppercorn mining plains, slowing past the sidings to glide into Spice Town Station, just as mum opened my bedroom door. I dived under the bed.

She shrieked, which brought my dad, 'Look at this! He's in the house. Tell me he isn't here.' She spun on her heels and stormed out of the room.

I knew what was coming next, 'I'll tan his backside when I catch him.'

I ran to Beth's. I saw she was with her father on the porch, sitting together on the swing. I ducked behind the bush to catch my breath before I joined them. I sat next to Beth and put my arm around her. She gave a little shiver then settled into my arm. Her dad was reading an excerpt from *To Kill a Mocking Bird* and, for a moment, I felt we were Atticus, Jem and Scout. Right then, we made the decision to study law.

I smile recalling how I morphed into a typical sloth

teenager, spending most of my time sleeping between bonking, eating and the occasional effort to study. Oh, and frustrating the hell out of my mum and dad by leaving the empty milk carton in the fridge and empty biscuit packets in the larder.

And yeah, okay. I didn't do a lot of bonking. Only wet dreams after nights studying late with Beth.

Dad and I started playing chess. Not together. When I happened past the chess set, I deigned to stop and make my move. Dad caught on and did the same.

I spent this afternoon with Beth. She concentrated on study, the exams are not far away. I fidgeted, trying to find the courage and right words to say. My plans went out the window and I blurted out, 'Beth, will you marry me?'

She's teasing me. She's going to give me her answer tomorrow, my birthday gift. To me, it will be life's gift.

I got to her front door to leave but at the last minute remembered to go back and pick up the centrepiece for the buffet table, a gift from her mum. I happened to overhear her speaking with her father. I snuck closer to the study until I could see her.

'Was he here today?' he asked.

'Yes, all afternoon. He's just left.'

'Have you made your mind up?'

I saw her nod. 'And, may I know your decision?'

'Yes. My decision is yes,' she said.

I ran out, containing my "whoop whoop' 'til I got behind the hedge.

Today's the day. Everything is ready for the celebrations. Waiting for the first guest to arrive, I take one last look at my train set, the steam train is still chugging its rhythmic tune, Choooo, Choo, ssst.

I hear the door open and go to meet everyone.

I reach for Mum and give her a big hug. Dad raises his hand; no handshake today, Dad. I hug him too. I turn to Beth and plant a soft but lingering kiss on her cheek.

I see a guy behind Beth. I can't recall meeting him before, but give him a smile and a nod of welcome. I raise an eyebrow when I see he is wearing a long white coat.

Oh no! Don't tell me you've hired a stripper. Please tell me he isn't a stripper.

He must have noticed the horror spread across my face and stepped forward. 'I need to check, one last time. You all agreed to go ahead?' he asked.

Dad said, 'Yes. Do it.' He turned to mum and nudged her, 'Love?'

Mum looked at my beautiful fiancé, who nodded. 'Yes,' she said.

'Yes,' Mum whispered as she took something from her bag and placed it on the table in front of me.

Bof's present. I nod. Yes, it is time to open it. I step

forward, loosen the catch, then flip back the lid. Two Chinese iron balls, adorned with intricate patterns, are nestled in a soft velvet cushion. I roll them under my fingertips, then pinch them together in short nips with my thumb and forefinger. We all smile at the sound of the bells hidden within their core.

I squint as the light in the room brightens to a sharp white light. I look up and take a step back. 'Bof?'

My grandfather smiles at me. 'Yes. It's your special birthday. I want to be with you.'

I caught a glimpse of movement; the stripper bent. I watch him pull at something, then he straightens, holding of all things, a power plug.

'What the ...?' I stutter. The Choooo, choo, ssst of my train stopped. 'He's turned my train off.'

I look at Mum. Her face holds a lopsided smile; tears run down her face; my father wipes away a tear. Beth, her arms around their shoulders, is staring at me with sad, moist eyes. They are all staring at me.

'Whoa? I don't understand. What's all this? What are you doing to me?'

My arms flail, fists clench, legs kick. *Hot, so hot.*

Free, I rise. Floating, I look down, see tubes and wires stuck into and on my still body.

I turn to Bof. He holds out his hand. I take it. At the same moment, I am blinded by an intense white light and sucked into a vortex.

I burst through the light, now suspended in the

ether. I face Bof, his body a shimmering translucent mercury.

'Are you up for an adventure?'

I nod and cease to exist, becoming one with the stars.

Acknowledgments

I was emboldened to bring this collection together by hearing comments from members of both the Scribblers Mandurah Murray Writers Group Inc and the Society of Women Writers WA, that they thought my stories were a really good read. So, I say thank you very much for your kind words, invaluable critiques and support.

Thank you to Brian and Anne Plowman, who allowed me to adopt Molly for a story.

Thank you to Helen Iles for your tireless commitment to assisting writers and for your publishing advice.

My partner, Di, simply said, 'Told you so.' Thank you, Di, for your unwavering support and love.

About the Author

Sandra was born and raised in the northeast of England and moved to Australia in 1979.

She lives in Mandurah, Western Australia, with her partner, Di, and their pampered pooch, Nelson.